Rattlebone

RATTLEBONE

MAXINE CLAIR

FARRAR, STRAUS AND GIROUX

NEW YORK

Library of Congress Cataloging-in-Publication Data
Clair, Maxine.
Rattlebone / Maxine Clair.—1st ed.
p. cm.
1. Afro-Americans—Kansas—History—20th century—Fiction.
2. Community life—Kansas—Fiction.
PS3553.L2225R37 1994   813'.54—dc20   93-50114   CIP

A different version of "October Brown" appeared in *Antietam Review*.

I am most grateful to the angel Jackie, wherever you are; Faye Moskowitz for her intuitive genius and unflagging encouragement; Katie for talking Spirit; my agent, Molly Friederich, for her levelheaded approach to miracles; Sara Bershtel for her editorial brilliance and painstaking love of process; Sally Singer for her valuable readings and suggestions; Stephen Bridges for helping me get the fonts right; David A. Anderson for *The Origins of Life on Earth*, his retelling of the Yoruba creation myth; the Maryland State Arts Council for their generous grant; and all the many others who blessed me with their good wishes.

For my first family—
Lucy and Robert Smith,
Robert, Jr., Gloria, Ronald,
Linda, Elinor, Joyce,
Donna and Steven

And always for Stephen, Michael, Joey and Adrienne
for this journey, this love

CONTENTS

OCTOBER
BROWN

W E HEARD IT from our friends, who got it from their near-eye-witness grandmothers and their must-be-psychic neighbor ladies, that when she was our same age, our teacher, Miss October Brown, watched her father fire through his rage right on into her mother's heart. In a fit of crazy-making grief, October Brown threw herself at walls and floors and cursed the name of God, apparently not mere blasphemy but mutterings that could cause limbs to crimp and men to yowl like jackals. The story went on that immediately thereafter, Satan himself had made a visitation to October Brown, and from that time until the year she became our grown-woman schoolteacher, the burnt brown of her left cheek was marked by a wavery spot of white: a brand, a Devil's kiss.

We put this together with what we already knew, which was that a patch of bleached skin meant death was on the way; the white would spread. When it covered your entire body you died.

I doubt that any of us fully believed every part of the story, but we were so seduced by the idea of it that before the end of the first day of school we buzzed with frenzy—a frenzy contained, because we imagined that a woman surrounded by such lore would have to have a bad temper, a flash fire that could drive her from her desk to yours in a single movement, dislodge you by your measly shoulders, plant you hard on the hardwood floor, tell you in growling underbreaths of wrath to stand up straight and say whatever she wanted you to say, and then crumble you in the mortar of her black-eyed stare.

Intuition is the guardian of childhood; it was keen in us, and we were right. Before we knew what current events were, she asked us who Wallis Warfield Simpson was and we sat. Attention shot through our arms and nailed our fists to the center of our desktops. Not a single hand went up.

Our eyes dared not follow her as she got up from her desk and moved around the room in a slow prance, falling back in her double-jointed knees like a camel with each step, around and around the room, asking "Who was Edward the Eighth?" speeding up while a few eyes shifted, a few feet shuffled under desks.

"Who knows or think they know?" she asked, and she was back at the desk again.

"All right, then, who was George the Sixth?"

We were still again, still until she whumped her *Thorndike International Dictionary* onto her desk and we grabbed our elbows.

"Look at me."

We looked.

"Who was George the Sixth?"

We looked, and the blue *Thorndike* flew over our heads and crashed into the back wall between two sixteen-paned windows. One corner pane of glass, weakened by BB shot some winter or summer before, fell to the radiator and shattered on the floor.

"Tomorrow I will ask you again."

My mother said that that was the nervy part of Miss Brown coming out, the Negro woman-teacher part of October Brown "trying to put some sense into y'all's pickaninny heads," she said.

"Tell your parents you will be learning French this year. Tell them to send a note if they want you to be excused from this part of your education." She went on: "These books are old but the rules have not changed. These books are special. Each one of these books belongs to me personally. You cannot buy one of these books or replace one, so govern yourselves accordingly." Then she said to John Goodson, "Pass these books out as far as they will go and share with your neighbors."

Never mind that the Kansas City curriculum did not include French, never mind that the Superintendent of Elementary Schools made threats against her for it. *"Qu'est-ce que c'est?" "C'est le pupitre." "Qu'est-ce que c'est?" "C'est la lumière."*

The unblemished side of Miss Brown shone on Wednesday afternoons after recess. "Class, put your heads down," she would say, and down went one overhead row of lights as she hushed her voice and read to our lowered heads about the time when everything was blacker than a hundred midnights and a lonely God stepped out on space, batting his lightning eyes, and made the world, made us out of mud by the river, and she read to our sleepy heads about boys going down a river on a raft, read to us in wherefore language about a boy and a girl, star-crossed, killing themselves accidentally and on purpose. She read aloud to herself and our curious heads listened, sneaking peeks of her perched on the side of her throne, legs wound round each other in long grace, her face a still, dark well of molasses, and death-kissed. Her coal-black hair carried all the life smells of her; parted in the middle, it hung in crowded crinkles to the shoulders of her shoulder-padded, to-the-nines dresses.

Those dresses. "I wouldn't wear nothin like that, but she got tiny hips," my mother said. They were draped at her waist or flounced, crepe with sequined dragons and peacocks, glittery butterflies, dresses that shone like the sun in the drab circle of dark clothes dark girls wore at the rear of the classroom, the place to which we gravitated at lunchtime, the back of the room where she graded papers, spread her napkin for her peeled boiled egg, peeled red tomato, her peeled-and-opened-like-a-flower orange on a white china plate aquamarine-trimmed. We nibbled, crust first, our baloney sandwiches and tried to match her spread on the waxed paper inside our fold-over-tuck paper pouches.

For all of us, staying at school for lunch meant being away from home all day, playing jacks, telling Hank Mizell stories. Hank was our recognized criminal who had stolen a dollar of the Defense Stamp money from Miss Brown's drawer and smuggled it out in his shoe. No one had told. Loyalty was hero-making, and from that day on, he was invincible.

But my mother said the Mizells had money enough to do anything they felt like doing. "Don't go gettin any notion in your head that you can do it too," she said, cross at me for no reason at all.

By a happenstance unclear to me then, my mother had steadily grown a baby inside her, aggravating my father in the process.

"What you think I am, Pearl, made of money? You better get your head out of the clouds and get some more ironin in here or somethin."

Whenever they talked, they talked about the baby. Whenever they didn't talk, it was about the baby too. For me they had only silence.

If you've ever tasted the after-rain clay dirt on a Kansas summer afternoon, or if you've ever secretly wanted to, you may understand why I was often tempted to eat a stick of chalk. It held the smell of that clay dirt. But if you had seen the overgrown girl that I was, standing dumb at the blackboard one day, sucking a stick of chalk, it might have seemed peculiar.

"Irene, what is wrong with you? Are you ill? Don't hunch your shoulders, answer yes or no," Miss Brown said.

I couldn't answer.

"If nothing is wrong, write your sums and be seated," she said.

That morning I had awakened to heat in my father's voice. "How many times do I have to tell you, Pearl? Stuff costs money! Since when can't you wash diapers? We didn't have no diaper service for Reenie."

And my mother's heat when she told him, "Don't start nothin with me, James. I'm the one havin this baby. Who got the last pair of shoes that come in this house? Answer me that. Who's all the time wearin me out about how his papa used to eat steak every Sunday?" My father tromped up the stairs. My mother tromped right behind him, not letting up.

They were on opposite ends of the same track, and I knew from time and again that they would both speed up, bear down until they had only inches left between them, then they would both fall back and rumble until silence prevailed. Later my father would bring home orange sherbet and my mother would rub his back and they would both be laughing.

But this time, before the rumble melted away, I heard what sounded like the whole house falling down. My father hollered out like he was using his last breath and ran down the steps. I flew to the top of the stairs. He was picking her up from the bottom, all the while praying, "Mercy." He yelled for me to call the home nurse on the phone, but when he saw that I couldn't move, he carried my mother to her bed and ran to call the nurse himself.

"Reenie, you wait by the door for the nurse," he told me, but I could not leave the foot of my mother's bed. Covering her with a quilt, he asked her *"please"* to be quiet, but she went right on nonstop about all the things she meant to order from the catalogue for the baby, all the places I could stay if they had to leave me alone. When the home nurse came, she told my mother and father that I should be sent along to school, but my father let me stay at home until they left for the hospital.

Certain that my mother's fall was preface to disaster, I stood there at the blackboard with the chalk in my mouth, sucking on the fact that one or the other, mother or baby, would die. I tried to focus my grief on the loss of the hump in my mother's belly but, unsure of my power to choose, I bit down on my mother gone.

"Irene, put the chalk down. You'd better sit and work on your word problems. What's the trouble?"

None of this escaped my friend Jewel Hicks, the pink-ribboned, talks-too-much, needs-her-butt-beat jewel daughter of the on-our-party-line Mrs. Hicks.

"Her daddy made her mamma fall down the steps and her mamma's going to have a baby."

Wailing is the sound you make to straighten out a tangled throat so that you can breathe, and to spill tears from boiling eyes so that you can see your "Come on, Irene" way out into the hall. Our janitor pushing his T-broom nodded, "How do, Miss Brown" in the dimness of the hallway, and the cedar-sawdust-muted-click of her high-heeled shoes comforted me as much as her arm around my shoulders all the way to the girls' restroom while I cried myself into hiccups.

"Now listen. No matter what happens, you are going to be all right," Miss Brown said. "You're a crackerjack, you're smart, and you can be strong even when you're afraid. But don't worry, your mother will be fine, the baby too, your daddy too."

When I got home from school that evening, my father had a guess-what lift in his voice and a halfway smile on his face.

"Of course your mamma wouldn't leave you and me like that," he told me. "And to boot," he said, "she got us a brand-new baby boy." I was the happiest girl in the Rattlebone end of Kansas City.

A few days later a baby came home with my mother. It was a tiny, raw-looking thing, writhing, gagging. At sudden times it drew up, spread tiny fingers, and grabbed at the air, shuddered as if it were falling. It squealed and fussed, and dirty clothes grew in mounds on the back porch. It slept, we listened to *Damon Runyon* and *Let's Pretend* with our ears stuck to the sides of the radio. It was the-baby-this, the-baby-that; it was practically Thanksgiving before things got back to normal.

By Christmastime Junie was sleeping all night and my mother had gone back to taking in ironing, ironing bushels of clothes. My father found masonry work indoors, all of us busy and tickled to be busy. A week before Christmas the Montgomery Ward truck pulled up in front of our house and we were immediately giddy. I knew some of the catalogue orders had to be mine. The driver brought several boxes to the door and my mother—"Step back, Reenie"—took them quickly to her room. Watching to see if that was all, I saw two men rolling a gleaming-white surprise down the plank to the sidewalk. I yelled so, my mother came running, then danced a piece of jitterbug when she saw it. "Westinghouse" it said. "Westinghouse!" I yelled. They sat it in the middle of the front room. "We needed it," my father said, grinning when he came home and my mother hung on his neck.

The double-wringer washing machine was a Mizells-ain't-got-nothin-on-us kind of thing, but I was even more ecstatic over my first store-bought, stitched-down pleated skirt, and knee socks to match. We were definitely coming up in the world.

WINTER ALWAYS ARRIVED before the sun was very far south in the sky, so that a white Thanksgiving was as unremarkable as jonquils ice-sheathed at Easter. A blizzard, though, was a drama that threatened to bring the house down. With a perverse exhilaration, we compared it to what we knew as ultimate devastation: the Atom Bomb.

Slate-gray clouds rumbled across the sky and exploded in needles of sleet. Then the all-day-all-night snow-wind screamed, whipping snow from place to place, unpredictably laying blank the railroad tracks and the cemetery, our outposts and borderlands, corners where we turned for home.

On the day of the storm, stuck at school, we were put out

about the fact that here we were, eight years old, and still had to wait for somebody's mamma to walk us home. In blizzards of previous years, the room mothers had always come bringing rainbow sandwiches—potted meat, cheese, and sweet relish layered on bread and cut into thin fingers—piled high on a platter for us to come up and take, one sandwich at a time. I remembered being secretly relieved to link my arms into two others and be part of a dark brood in make-do headgear that followed William's mother to the early light of our own porches, where we were handed over to our own mothers.

Jewel's mother swept in and bundled up her sweet one, Hank's uncle came to take everyone who lived on Wynona. No sandwiches arrived, though John Goodson's father did bring vanilla wafers. Pancakes of snow slid down panes of glass, then dribbled into the double-cardboard pane and dripped onto the radiator. I watched.

This once was the only time my father ever came to school, and he didn't merely show up; he kicked the classroom door hard from the outside. When Miss Brown opened it, my father stood snow-weighted in his black-and-red mackinaw and hunting cap, holding an orange crate lined with an army blanket. "Hi," he said to her. He was grinning. She turned away without speaking, without finding anything to do with her eyes.

"The room mothers sent this—there's enough chili in there to feed all y'all," he said.

Miss Brown shook out the blanket and lifted my mother's canning pot from the crate, then boxes of crackers, Dixie cups, streamers of paper-wrapped, figure-eight wooden spoons. O happy day! Single file, we got our cups filled and sat down to eat wherever we liked.

At the back of the room Miss Brown spread my father's

mackinaw on the radiator, steaming and burning wool. My father sat big on top of the last desk in one row; Miss Brown sat smaller on another, across the aisle, facing him, and they talked while we ate our chili.

She peeled her orange, dangled her legs in the aisle. She held it out to him, a flower offering on a china plate. He shook his head no. She ate one section, cherry-slick fingertips into cherry-red lips, so proper. My father talked. He reached for a piece of her orange. She talked. She talked. He talked. Leaning over, she laughed and her heavy, live, crinkled hair fell forward and covered her face. She looked eyes-through-hair at him. She snapped straight and threw the mass of hair back, held it back with both hands, spreading elbows angel-winged out into the air. Letting go of her hair, she shook it into place and crossed her legs, talking, talking.

Smiling, she touched the many-colored, parrot-appliquéd shoulder of her dress. Smiling, my father showed teeth all-around white. A pretty dress. Black, crepe, French. She arched herself, swung her legs, girl on a swing. When my father stood up to go, he slid his arms into her holding of his mackinaw. She held the door—"Bye, James"—for us.

No matter how fast he walked, I kept one step behind him, deep in his footprints down Sherman Alley and out Lenexa. Though he carried the box, he never slowed down. I passed him on the turn into the narrow path of our street and tried to run, feet stinging, home. After all the rush, I had nothing to say to my mother, who sang to me her rendition of Nat "King" Cole's "Sweet Lorraine" over my feet, cold in the basin—*Just found joy, he's as happy as a baby boy, with another brand-new choo-choo toy, now he's found his sweet Irene, Irene, Irene.*

If winter seemed definite, desperate, then spring seemed timid, capricious, like an innocent girl feigning wisdom. One day you felt a near-balmy wind, or sensed an almost-perfume from crocuses, saw the perhaps-violet six-o'clock sky and you guessed it was spring.

I was mostly indifferent to it. Something had invaded our house. I watched my mother's belly.

"Don't be ridiculous, girl, I almost got my waist back," she said.

That wasn't it. Still, a no-name, invisible something had settled on us. For instance: I saw it in the way nothing suited my father.

"Pearl, can't you think of nothin to cook but neckbones? The stuff tastes like homemade sin. Ain't we got nothin sweet but pound cake?" he would say.

He was impatient with Junie—"Keep that boy quiet or git him outta here." Or careless with my mother's feelings—"You look like who'da-thought-it in that dress." Or he was absent, playing whist somewhere late at night with people my mother called God-knows-who.

I heard it in the way my mother said "Reenie, be quiet" or "Talk up, girl" or "You shoulda been through cookin by now. Play with your brother." She'd stay behind her bedroom door for hours, and come out with her eyes puffy.

She cried, she said, for my grandmother who had died when I was four. She cried, she said, for my uncle who was in Korea. For Junie's rash, the burn on her ironing hand, a hole in my sock. For nothing, she said. "Nothin is wrong."

But it was there.

Too early, before bird-twitter one morning, I heard my father's brogans shuffling, my mother's voice breaking in ways

I held my ears against. Doors and drawers slammed, their voices peaked and sprawled, jabbed through the floor and walls.

When my father's heavy boots thundered all the way to the front door and down the walk without sounding even for a second like he was turning around, I ran to my window. In a morning light that was like gray gauze, I saw him swing a large suitcase into the cab of his truck.

I could barely hear my voice ask why. My mother could barely say, "Just for a while."

Counting the days, I tried living the fantasy of my father away on a trip. But evenings, just before dark, when all the neighborhood seemed to settle inside kitchens and I sat alone at our table watching my mother—her whole dinner between two slices of bread—stand at the window and eat slowly into night, I knew that my father was gone.

At first he stayed away, but eventually he took to stopping by to bring money or groceries or just himself for us to see. My mother always got busy in the kitchen or upstairs and left me to wonder out loud why and where and how much longer he would be wherever he was living, and who was fixing his dinner.

"Wait now, Reenie," he said. "That's for me and your mamma to talk about." But he told me that no matter where he lived, when school was out, he would still take me with him to pick wild greens and he would still teach me how to tell the good mushrooms from the bad ones. It was relieving to hear, but the end of school was like eternity, something I could not imagine.

On Sundays my father ate dinner with us. After dinner, when he fell asleep on the divan with Junie in a snoozing bundle on his chest, my mother and I watched, ostensibly sewing and doing homework, but watching what could be if we could somehow fasten up the life we'd had together.

Then one morning I took a shortcut through the hollow and when I arrived at school early, I saw a blue flatbed truck just like my father's pulling away from the curb and Miss Brown going into the building. I thought to call out, but the man in the truck was wearing a felt hat with a brim, the kind men wore to church. My father had only a hunting cap. Besides, I reasoned, my father had to be at work long before I had to be at school; it could not be him.

At about this time, school seemed pointless. Easter came and went and not even my new linen pleated skirt could cheer me. I relinquished my crackerjack seat and gave up my friendship with Jewel, so when we made our annual school jaunt to the Nelson Gallery of Art in three church buses with room mothers and teachers keeping a lid on our bubbling enthusiasm, I must have been ripe for the new taking-over of my mind.

In the days that followed, I took to drawing. For no reason I drew trees. Naked winter trees, charcoal black on white paper. Trees with no buds, no leaves. Trees whose roots went down to the tip of nothingness, trees held in place only by the space on the white page. "Spring fever," Miss Brown said. I drew fragile roots and branches in the margins of incomplete homework, badly done test papers.

"Tell me what's gotten into you, Irene," she said. I studied less and drew more trees, and she slashed the trees with red X's, asked me about my falling-asleep-with-my-eyes-open look. I drew more and she made me redo the work neatly. I drew black trees instead of redoing my work and she kept me near her desk and monitored my papers, asked me none-of-your-business things about my mother and father.

It rained. It rained more. And on one of those rainy afternoons that we stayed in for recess, Miss Brown left the room. Hank Mizell, digging through the bowels of the supply closet, came up with the box of Kotex Miss Brown reserved for intimate female catastrophes. With all eyes coaxing, he splashed red tempera down the middle of one napkin. Miss Brown opened the door at just the right time to catch him in the not-even-a-prayer position of placing it on her chair.

"Out!" She grabbed for his arm. He dodged.

"You better not touch me," he said.

She grabbed again, faster this time, and caught his arm.

"I said out of here!" And she pointed to the door.

"Get your hands offa me, you black sidditty bitch! My mamma said you're a whore." And Hank fixed his eyes on me. Miss Brown looked at me too, then fixed her eyes on him.

Her look carried such fury we could all feel the silent curse she singed him with before she spun and pranced head-high out the door, her smeared Devil's kiss glowing pink. Hank shrunk and slinked out behind her. I ran to the doorway and watched them, hen and duckling, down the length of the hallway and into the office.

The next day, rumor billowed that Hank's mother was coming to school to straighten the whole thing out. Hank Mizell's family owned the funeral home, and as hoity-toity as his mother was in protecting their name, she was deaf, mute, and blind when it came to Hank. We were excited. According to our Jewel, Hank had told his mother that Miss Brown had slapped him, said it happened on the way to the office, said she made the scratch he was sporting. His mother was coming to take Miss Brown to the Board, Jewel said. The almighty, no-corporal-punishment-allowed Board of Education.

THE PRINCIPAL LOOKED pressed. "Who saw what happened between Miss Brown and Hank Mizell?"

Every hand went up.

"Who would like to come with me to the office to discuss it?"

Every hand went down.

More tense, she pressed. "John Goodson?"

"I don't remember all of it," he said.

"Jewel Hicks?"

"My mother said that I should stop telling everything I know," she said.

"Irene?"

I was silent.

"In my office, Irene."

In the office they all sat in a semicircle in front of the principal's desk. On one end Miss October Brown sat erect in an armchair, with both high-heeled feet on the floor, looking through a *Weekly Reader* as though she was alone in the office. She folded the paper and folded her arms. Then Hank Mizell's mother. She wore a whole fox around her shoulders, its beady eyes open in my direction. She held Hank's hand over the arm of her chair. Then Hank, hunched and cramped in his mother's hold. Then the janitor, hunched too.

"Sit down, Irene," the principal said.

I smoothed the pleats down the back of my linen skirt and sat carefully on them.

The principal said, "I want all of you to know that we're

here simply to get to the bottom of this matter. I don't have to tell you that we can do this quickly if each of you will just relate the truth." And she sat down behind her desk.

"Henry, would you like to begin by telling us what happened yesterday?"

"Yes, ma'am," Hank said. His story included being caught out of his seat even though it *was* recess, being yanked by the arm that was still sore, being frightened enough to swear, and being slapped.

"She slapped me upside my head hard, and her fingernails are sharp," he said. "They scratched me."

Miss Brown crossed her legs and folded her hands in her lap. Hank Mizell's mother looked at the cherry-red nails and sighed the sigh of the wronged.

"Miss Brown?" the principal said.

"First, let me just remind all of you," Miss Brown said, "that this is not the first time Henry Mizell has been guilty of unacceptable conduct, nor is this the first lie he has ever told."

"I beg your pardon," Hank's mother said. "You don't talk like that about my son with me sitting right here. I don't have to be subjected to this."

"Please, Mrs. Mizell, let's let Miss Brown finish." The principal wrung her hands as Miss Brown told her story, which involved her instructions to the class about staying in their seats whenever they were using paint, her shock about the sanitary napkin and the name calling.

"I did touch his arm to restrain him for a moment because he broke to run," she said. "But other than that, I did nothing corporal to him whatsoever."

The janitor spoke without looking up. "You know," he said, "y'all ought to have some way these children can play inside.

They need to run when they been cooped up all day or they gonna get into trouble. The boy was wrong, but look like to me he needed to move around some, and seem like the teacher did too. Maybe if y'all—"

The principal interrupted. "Did you see Miss Brown and Henry in the hallway yesterday?"

"I sho'nuff did."

"Did you see Miss Brown do anything? I mean to Henry."

"Naw, ma'am, I didn't. But you know, these eyes is gettin old and there ain't enough light out there. I think I'da heard him, though, if she really whopped him. Course, maybe he didn't say nothin. Maybe he was scared."

We were all quiet for a while.

"Irene?" the principal said softly. All their eyes turned to me. I watched my hands unfold in my lap and smooth my pleats. I looked at Miss Brown looking her I'm-proud-of-you look at me. I looked at the principal, and though my mouth was very dry and my hands very quivery, though my heart was whooshing hard in my ears, I looked her straight in the eye the way people do when they are telling the truth.

"Yes," I said. "She did." I said level and clear, "She hit him."

"Irene!" Miss Brown stood up. Her Devil's kiss glowed fire-red as it always did when her temper flared. But she sat down slowly.

"Go on, Irene," the principal said.

"Just before they got to the office," I said, "she turned around and slapped him. I could see them from the door," I said. "I guess she lost her temper because he called her a vulgar name."

"Are you sure, Irene?" the principal said. I nodded yes.

"Well, that's all I need to know to take this up elsewhere," Hank's mother said.

"Mrs. Mizell, I believe we can handle this right here if Miss Brown is willing to apologize," the principal said. But Hank's mother said, "No thank you, I'm tired of having to come down here every other time somebody gets it in their mind to take their jealousy out on Henry." And she stood up to leave.

Miss Brown picked up the purse beside her chair, stuck it under her arm—"The children are lying"—and headed for the door.

"Please wait," the principal said to Miss Brown and Hank's mother. "Irene, you're excused."

Instead of going directly back to class, I headed for the restroom, where I tucked in my blouse, braided the ends of my braids, and washed my hands in castile. I folded my knee socks all the way down and sat on the cool radiator. A breeze played in the narrow opening of the frosted window, and I raised the window higher to look out.

Spring was unraveling everywhere. Summer was coming when I would go hunting for wild greens with my father, when we would be up in the warm, damp mornings taking his gunnysack with us along the railroad tracks all the way to the woods. Summer was coming when he would show me which was dandelion and which was dock, which was pokeberry and which was nettle. We would bring back morels and truffles for my mother to dip in egg and crackers and fry them crispy brown. Summer was coming and maybe my father would come back. Maybe he would buy orange sherbet every night. Maybe my mother would get her waist back and sew herself a princess-line dress. Maybe she would sew us both one of the new kind of skirts cut on the bias so they flared way out and you never had to worry about keeping the pleats straight.

LEMONADE

THE SATURDAY-MORNING-ONLY milkman who brought the new, homogenized bottles from Armourdale. The here-he-comes whose only name was Insurance Man, except for that one time on Mr. Mozelle's porch when he said something that made Mr. Mozelle draw back his fist before Mrs. Mozelle could stop him. Doll leaning on the register at Doll's Market, taking our pennies for B-B Bats and baloney by the slice. Mr. always-quiet Heltzberg bent in a stout C and carrying his stained leather satchel—thick with sheet music—on the shelf of his back every Wednesday afternoon by bus from way out in doo-waditty to Wanda's house and back to the bus stop. In the Rattlebone end of Kansas City, those were our white people.

Then *she* drove up in a raggedy-trap, old-time car with no top, black slits in the side of the hood, running boards, rumble seat stuffed with what looked like broken furniture, and a horn blasting Aah-hooga! Aah-hooga!

She stepped out of the car, unfolding her flat self to be taller than any of our mothers. Except for her face, all of her was covered up in white: a long-sleeved, church-ushering dress, white nurse's shoes, white stockings, white gloves, white thing twist-wrapped around her head with no hair showing. She was the whitest—not beige, not pink, not rouge or lipstick—white woman we had ever seen.

Janey, Cece, Deb, Wanda, Wanda's big brother Puddin, and I had been playing Lemonade, and it was Wanda's turn to be the star:

> *Here I come.*
> > *Where you from?*
> *New Orleans.*
> > *What's your trade?*
> *Lemonade.*
> > *Get to work and show us something.*

Wanda was just about to get to work and show us the splits when we broke up our audience on the corner and lined up on the curb. Since Doll's car had already cruised away for the night, and since the dusk had grown thick enough for the streetlight—our spotlight—to come on, we knew this coming-in-our-neighborhood was an unusual thing.

"Hi, girlies," she said. Everyone looked at me because, though Wanda was the oldest, I was the tallest. I said, "Hi."

"I'm Miss Joan," she said, "and I have a very special little show in my car. Would you all like to see it?"

"Not me," I said. I did want to see if she had one of those Junior League puppet shows we had seen at school, but this was a stranger's car and we were not to go near it.

"Not me," Puddin said, only it came out *Naa-mee.* He never just up and said anything on his own except when he got mad, and then we could only guess at what he was trying to say.

"What is it? What you got?" Wanda asked.

Instead of answering, she asked us for our names.

"Me, I'm Wanda Coles. What you got to show us?"

"I'm Janey."

"I'm Cecelia Mozelle."

"My name is Irene Wilson, but my nickname is Reenie," I said. "And that's Puddin. Say *Puddin*," I said to him. He tried, but as usual it came out *Bud*.

"What's the matter with him?" Miss Joan asked us.

"Nothing. He's my big brother, but he can't talk too good," Wanda said. "What's that in the back of your car?"

"Is he a mongoloid?" Miss Joan asked.

People were always asking what was wrong with Puddin, but nobody ever called him a mongoloid. All I knew was that Puddin and Wanda Coles had lived across the corner from us forever and that Puddin was different. He was sixteen or seventeen, but you couldn't tell it because he didn't know how to talk or put his clothes on straight, or do anything else the way we could. Once when the police brought him home from breaking the window in Doll's store, they called him a crazy, purple blankety-blank and tried to make him talk. Doll had refused to press charges and the police were upset that they couldn't arrest him. My mother got so furious that Puddin's mother had to tell her to just go on back into the house before the police started in on her.

"Hello, Pudding," Miss Joan said, and Puddin stared at her with his blank face and smooth, round head.

Without another word she pulled an easel out of the rumble seat, set a large, framed square of white cloth on the easel, and began to fill in the white space with contours of colored felt—green felt at the bottom for the earth, dark blue at the top for the night sky, and one great star with jewel-cloth rays slanting down from one corner. Miraculously the felt pieces stayed in place once she rubbed them with her white-gloved hand. By the time she placed paper cutouts of two cows and a donkey, I knew this was shaping up to be a Little-Town-of-Bethlehem scene, and June wasn't even over yet.

"Do you know who this is?" she asked, pointing to a cutout of a manger-baby with real dried grass stuffed around it.

"That's baby Jesus," Debra said.

"And who's this?" It was a cutout kneeling near the manger.

"That's Jesus' father," Debra said.

"And do all of you know who this is?" she asked, looking around at us.

Wanda rolled her eyes, sighed, then blurted out, "*That's* Mary, *that's* Joseph, and *that's* the manger for the shepherd boy to come to—if you've got a shepherd boy—and Magi from the East are about to bring him some gold, myrrh, and frankincense, which not too many people had heard of a long time ago."

And Wanda pointed. "You need an angel right up there to tell Joseph that he has to get out of Bethlehem before Herod kills Jesus. He killed all the boys anyhow. And you need—"

"I wasn't going in that direction," Miss Joan said. "I want to go back, before Jesus was born, to talk about Mary, the mother of God. Now this is the angel Gabriel, who told Mary that she was going to be the mother of Our Lord."

Miss Joan stood with her back to the car, feet close together and pointer in hand. She proceeded to tell us all about how Gabriel assured Mary that she would become a blessed person by being the mother of Jesus, and just as Miss Joan got going good about how Mary's friend, Elizabeth, was the mother of

John the Baptist, my mother came out on the porch and called me.

Our visitor folded her paper dolls and easel, the felt earth and starry sky, and said it was time for her to go. As she pulled away from our curb, we all tagged each other and split up in homeward directions. Except for Puddin. My mother let him sit alone on our steps dipping his finger into the jar of mayonnaise that he liked as much as we liked ice cream. When the cicadas stopped singing and his mayonnaise was all gone, my mother watched him saunter across the street, home.

"What was that lady selling?" My mother asked me that night while she cleaned my ear with her baby finger.

"She was trying to tell us Bible stories," I said. "I guess she doesn't know too many since all she showed us was Christmas."

A FEW DAYS later, when Miss Joan came by again, the light already shone its round spotlight on the brick street where we were in the midst of hide-and-go-seek. And this time when she chugged up and climbed out wearing her same outfit, she said we should call her Joan of Arc. *Sister* Joan of Arc. From what I knew, Joan of Arc was a soldier-kind-of-girl who burned at the stake because everybody in her backward country thought she was a witch. Therefore, at least in my estimation, this new Joan of Arc was looking to be famous in the same way. That kind of desire was beyond me. Immediately, she began talking about Mary again, whom she called Queen of Heaven, Our Lady, the Blessed Virgin. She told us a story of the time several Portuguese children saw Mary in a vision while they watched their sheep.

Wanda said, "If I saw the ghost of Mary, I wouldn't be scared."

"If you ever see a vision of Mary," Sister Joan said, "it will be a sign that you are surely one of the chosen ones."

By the time we repeated the Lord's Prayer her way—leaving off *For thine is the kingdom*, because she said Jesus didn't really say that part—and then said a prayer to Mary over and over, I thought we might be in trouble. She told us to pray like this every night and every morning, but this sounded too much like the chant we sometimes heard when we had a holiday but the white girls at St. Theresa's—the church and school in back of Cece's grandmother's house—had to go to school. Over and over they said prayers to statues, which everybody knew was a sin. I knew my mother would have a fit if she knew we were putting some other god before God, even if it was Jesus' mother.

"God is jealous," my mother used to say. "He can whip you worse than any power on this earth can, so don't you go trying Him."

We were definitely bordering on trying Him. And besides, we were supposed to call grown folks by Miss and Missus and Mister. We had plenty of Sisters and Brothers and Mothers at our church, but only the grown folks were allowed to say Sister So-and-so, Mother Thus-and-such. We were asking for it.

Needless to say, I didn't tell my mother about Miss Joan's new name or about the prayers, and when my mother asked, I said merely that we had heard more Bible stories.

"What's she doing coming around here, anyway?" my mother asked herself while she finished the dishes. "Ain't she got nothing better to do at night except bother y'all?" she said aloud the next day while she plaited my hair. "Wonder why she wears all that white," she muttered while she munched her sardines and crackers.

I thought Sister Joan of Arc must have gotten wind of my mother's temperament and decided to let us Tenth Street children alone. For the long while that we didn't see her, I went back to saying the regular end of the Lord's Prayer without thinking about her. We went back to playing lemonade, with me winning for the best show because I learned all of my father's Nat "King" Cole records and because I did the wind-up jive better than Cece and Wanda. Of course Wanda griped about cheating because she couldn't haul her piano out to the corner and win by playing "The Skater's Waltz," the only song she knew, the only one she ever talked about.

One Wednesday evening, on his way to the bus stop, Mr. Heltzberg stopped by our corner and asked me if my mother was home. He knocked on our screen door and talked for a long time before my mother let him into our house. I went around to the back door to listen.

He was telling my mother that Mrs. Coles, Wanda's mother, had said I was musical, and that perhaps I could take piano lessons. When they had given piano lessons at the church, I didn't take them because I wasn't allowed to practice on the church piano every day. Mr. Heltzberg said that Mrs. Coles told him I could practice every day on theirs, that Wanda was becoming uninterested, that maybe I would push her. My mother said she would think about it.

"If I do let you go over there," she told me, "you have to act like you got some home training and don't go wandering through their house looking at all their things. And I don't want you eating over there, either," she said. "They got sugar diabetes in that house."

And so I took piano lessons with Mr. Heltzberg every Wednesday at five o'clock at the Coles cata-corner house that smelled like mayonnaise.

BY THE TIME we saw Sister Joan of Arc again, I had been taking piano lessons for a few weeks and practicing every day. Sometimes when both Wanda and me were finished practicing, Puddin would sit down and hit a note repeatedly, hard, with one finger until he took us to the brink of nutty, and we'd hold his hands and tell him Sister Joan of Arc was coming. Her name seemed to do the trick. We couldn't tell whether he feared her, or hoped to see her, or had no clue to what we were saying. Yet it kept his finger from its one-note concerto.

Nor was I clear in my own fear-or-fascination for her. The evening she reappeared in all her whiteness, she pulled out yet another marvelous thing. From a red velvet pouch, one by one she handed each of us a necklace of beads with a cross attached.

Now the beads were just beads, black and not all that attractive. But the cross on the end? By its size I knew it had to be for warding off formidable evil. I thought I knew a little bit about evil. For instance, there were the Red Quanders, those strange, African people who wrapped their heads with bright red scarves and wore long wrap-dresses or braided beards and raised most of their own food in a small section of Rattlebone near the railroad tracks. They could work black magic, which, according to everyone I knew, was inspired by the Devil. And there was that other, stronger evil your unknown enemies could bring to you. Once when my aunt had man trouble, then female trouble, then lost the maid-work job she had with the rich Websters who made her eat plain white spaghetti for lunch, my mother thought something was amiss. Things were so bad for my aunt that she had to bring my cousins to live with us for the school year. My aunt was sure that somebody had gotten some of her hair from her hairbrush, or one of her runned stockings out of her trash. My mother told my aunt to bury a cross right where my aunt's porch steps met the sidewalk. Soon after that, my aunt got work at another family's house where they gave her ham for lunch and nice gifts at Christmas.

I knew that this large cross that Sister Joan offered was designed to ward off more evil than I ever planned to come across. It was a power I didn't want to take into my own hands. Sister Joan of Arc insisted, though, that we needed protection from any-and-everything. She put the black-beaded charm around Puddin's neck, saying that a mongoloid needed it especially. She took us through the Lord's Prayer again with the short ending, had us say the Hail-Mary prayer a few times, the Holy-Mary-Mother-of-God prayer a few times and gave each of us a small, black book of prayers. She made us hold on to the rosary and swear that, counting off the beads, we would say these prayers every morning and every night.

Wanda shook her head. "My mother don't want me doing that," she said.

The rest of us gave the same testimony.

"That's all right," Sister said. "You can do it quietly. You don't have to say them aloud. Someday your mothers will be glad."

Although I took the beads, I couldn't imagine my mother being glad. I should have known that this same mother who knew when I sang the wrong note in "The Old Rugged Cross" during our Easter Sing, and who found out that I used strong language like *black lie* and *hell* at school anytime I felt like it —I should have known that she would find out that Sister Joan of Arc not only gave us rosaries, but that she looped a black-beaded-charm around Puddin's neck that would probably work something terrible on him.

THEN A STRANGE thing happened. It began when Mr. Heltzberg suggested that if I kept doing well, he would teach me the bass part to "The Skater's Waltz" so that Wanda and I could play a duet. I couldn't wait to practice harder, but the following Wednesday when Mr. Heltzberg arrived, Wanda said she hated piano and that I should just go on and take her practice time since I had already mooched in on her lessons, to which Mrs. Coles said Wanda had better just get used to the competition, to which Mr. Heltzberg made a nervous explanation about his duet-idea and nearly swallowed one of his horehound drops trying to get the words out in the right order.

"Lizzen to me," he said. "Chust lizzen," and he sat down on Wanda's piano stool and started to play a song with all kinds of notes way up and way down the piano. He sounded better than the radio. While Wanda and I and Puddin and Mrs. Coles watched, he closed his eyes, skated his stubby fingers over the white and black keys as easily as I could dust a shelf.

When he finished we were quiet. "Sonata," he said. "You two vill do dat." Wanda and I saw him to the door and watched him haul his satchel to the bus stop.

We were on her front porch trying to outdo each other with apologies when we heard someone playing the exact same piece Mr. Heltzberg had just played. We ran inside. There, sitting on the stool with his smooth-brown, blue-tongued, shave-headed impossible self was Puddin, eyes front, playing away. Mrs. Coles, coming to see why Mr. Heltzberg was still there, immediately lost her breath and leaned against the wall.

"Go get your mamma!"

I ran across the street yelling "Mamma!" so wildly that Cece's mother two doors down came out and followed my mother along with my cousins Bea and Eddy, the mailman Mr. Eugene, Mrs. Mozelle and Cece, Deb and her brother, Mrs. Lydia Pemberton, who owned the rooming house and was in the neighborhood selling dinners for the church, even the Red Quander egg man came to the door. All of us except the egg man crowded into Wanda's front room, holding hands and listening to Puddin play *Moonlight Sonata, Moonlight Sonata*, over and over again.

Right on through the moments that Wanda's mother wiped her tears on her dress, and the happy moment Miss Lydia got on the line and ordered six free fish dinners from the church, and the unbelievable moment Mr. Eugene threw up ticker-tape handfuls of neighborhood mail, Puddin played. All while Wanda found seats for everyone and poured Kool-Aid, Puddin played. After a while, Wanda's mother said she guessed that that was enough for now.

"Okay, honey, we thank the Lord, but you can stop now," she said. "Puddin, honey," she said, "you can do it again later, I know you can," and he played on. Finally and gently she tried to lift his hands, but his fingers were wired to the keys as he played on.

"Oh-oh," Wanda said. "Puddin ain't stoppin." Then she said, "Come on," and I knew what she was thinking. We went upstairs and up to the attic where from under her bed she pulled out a wadded bandanna. On the way down, she untied it and let the necklace of beads dangle from the high-held cross.

"Sister Joan of Arc is coming!" she said in front of everybody, and waved the cross. I lifted Puddin's hands from the keys. Eyes widened as Wanda's mother ran to the kitchen, and by the time she returned with a spoon and jar of mayonnaise, everyone had collected themselves and disappeared.

Since my mother needed time to think about the afternoon's events, pray about them, talk them out with Cece's grandmother, who sometimes helped with the cooking at St. Theresa's Convent, Wanda and I walked down to Doll's Market to get us a strawberry B-B Bat. And since things work in mysterious ways that we can never figure, Wanda and I saw Sister Joan of Arc's car parked there. We found Her Whiteness in Doll's store, at Doll's cold-box without a glove, turning up a bottle of Coca-Cola.

"Well, here they are," Doll said. "We heard all about Puddin."

"You blessed girls," Sister said.

Doll continued. "The whole neighborhood is talking about it. I never heard of such, but far be it from me to say it's impossible. You all know this here lady?"

"Hi, Sister Joan of Arc," I said, feeling like I should curtsy.

"Where is the boy?"

"He's home, but I don't think my mamma's going to let him play the piano anymore today," Wanda said.

"So it is true," Sister Joan said. "You see, the Blessed Virgin is smiling in your lives. See how she loves you. You must consider it a blessing that you were privileged to witness this miracle."

Then she took my hands in hers—one hand cold, the other warm in its soft glove—and stooped to bore her eyes into my face. Up close I could see the pale yellow where her hair began along the edge of her turban, the pale yellow lashes on the pink line of eyelids around pale, steady, gray marbles, the pale pink inside her lips that moved slowly, deliberately, when she said, "Our Lady needs girls like you to do her work on earth. I'll take you home."

She assumed we would ride in her big car the three blocks home, but once outside, Wanda and I were not about to climb in. We told her that we didn't want to get sticky candy on her nice seats, and that we'd rather walk. She drove ahead to wait at our corner.

From a distance, we could see the noisy group around her car. I knew my mother's shape and hair. Half the neighborhood was there, including Wanda's mother, Cece's mother, and Puddin. Sister Joan of Arc stood like the Queen of Heaven in the car, taller than ever, pronouncing pronouncements, presenting with her arms, clasping her hands, repeatedly making the sign of the cross. Wanda and I ran to hear what they all had to say.

"Just look at what has happened!" Sister Joan was saying. "You think this poor retarded boy could have done what he did without me? I tell you, I said the rosary for him every day and now he can make music. You have Our Lady to thank for it. She has interceded on his behalf. And the Holy Mother can save all of your children if you just give them to her. Let me take them to mass . . ."

"Say what you want," my mother said. "We don't have nothing against Mary, but God and only God has the kind of power you're talking about. My child cut her teeth on the Word, so there ain't a whole lot you can tell her that she don't already know. The thing is, I'm her mamma. If there's going to be any recruiting, recruit me. Look *me* in the eye and tell me I don't know nothing about God."

Sister Joan said, "Well I'm sure you know something about God, but obviously you don't know the *truth*."

My mother flinched.

Sister Joan went on. "And that is fine. You have chosen your life. But these children. 'Suffer the little children to come unto Me, for such . . .' "

My mother cut in. "You all over there in that church can strut and chant and sashay around in robes all you want to, talking Latin like God don't understand English, and telling those priests all your business. But what makes you think you got a duty to come over here and collect *our* children?"

"Tell her, Pearlean," Wanda's mother put in.

Sister Joan folded her hands and looked down at them. "I am *trying* . . . to *save* . . . their *souls*," she said. "If you would just listen, you could learn something about bringing them up to honor the Holy Mother, not to ignore her emissaries."

"Let me tell you something, Sister Emissary," Cece's mother said. "You had better let God save their souls and you stick to saving your behind while you still got it. Don't let me get started."

Sister Joan lifted a huge wooden cross out of the pocket of her white dress and began hailing Holy Mary. As my mother and the others went on trying to talk to her, she got louder, and the louder she got, the more our mothers went on. Finally Sister Joan got so loud that she was yelling, beseeching the angels, "Holy Michael Archangel, defend us in the day of battle . . ."

"Don't let us have to snatch that rag from around your head and tie it around your mouth, Sister!" Cece's mother said.

"That's enough now, y'all," my mother said, and took Cece's mother's arm. "She can stand out here all night yelling to high heaven if she wants to. We don't have to listen."

They turned away from the car, and Sister Joan, with her eyes still closed, piped down a little.

For one last warning my mother turned and said, "The next time you see a bunch of kids tending to their business and leaving yours alone, you'd best keep chugging your little wagon right on through here. Only God is God, and only *this* holy mother is going to tell my child what is what."

"Put that in your pipe and smoke it!" Cece's mother said.

"Irene, you and Bea get on in the house."

"You too, Wanda."

As we went in, we heard Sister Joan crank up her car. It was the last we ever saw of her. For a long time afterward, although I had surrendered my rosary to my mother, I continued to daydream about a miracle that would make me sing like Sarah Vaughan. Until we could suck no more juice from them, the thwarted-missionary stories we overheard rattled in our heads with the escapee-from-Osawatomie stories we made up. Wanda and I sorted out all of the facts Cece gave us straight from her grandmother about how Sister Joan of Arc bore no resemblance to real nuns. What did Cece's grandmother know? Wasn't it possible that Sister Joan of Arc had been a nun, and that the convent had sent her away because they caught her drinking from a bottle, say, or looking at herself in a mirror, or maybe even kissing a priest?

We were shocked at quiet Mr. Heltzberg's know-it-all attitude when he told our mothers how a man-boy like Puddin could have some secret thing in his brain that could make him do something that grand. It got so, Mr. Heltzberg loved throwing his "Now you vill hear Bach" and "Now you vill hear Rachmaninoff" business out to us as he raced up and down Wanda's piano, smiling at Puddin, who had no better sense than to stand there with his hand stuck in a mayonnaise jar.

As summer rolled on, we kept up the game of lemonade. Perhaps none of us would ever come up with anything as spectacular as what Puddin had done. But every gray dusk in the dim wash of streetlight, I continued to pop my fingers, boogying across my corner, trying to win.

WATER

SEEKS ITS

OWN LEVEL

THIS IS WHAT he saw: two muddy rivers coursing toward each other, rushing as if they were drawn by the axis of a great Y, then their headlong crash and the furious confusion over which river would prevail. Beyond this junction, the Kaw ceased to exist, and the Missouri flowed on. Such tides were not easily turned.

All day James Wilson had sat on the steps outside Union Hall, waiting to be sent on a job. Any job. But preferably to the subdivision in Olathe where, for several months, Cordon Construction had been laying foundations, and he had been bricking them in. The pay was good. Better than good. But the white boys were getting even better than that. Two days earlier he had protested—not so respectfully—the foreman's scheme of sending all the men home and letting the white boys sneak back for overtime. He admitted to himself that if he could have just ignored it, just let it go, he would be working in Olathe instead of standing on a hill in Rattlebone watching the river rise.

The long whine of the late-shift whistle from Armour's packing house stirred him. He was sure it was only a little past six. He took in the Kansas City smell of manure and bacon, strongest in Rattlebone across and downriver from the stockyards. For the late whistle to blow now meant that the workers were quitting early—locking pens, switching off conveyor belts, and hurrying home. At Union Hall all afternoon radios had broadcast warnings to the low-lying communities along the rivers. Evacuations were imminent, the levee might not hold. Since Rattlebone was on high ground, it was probably safe, but James thought he ought to be heading home too. He went down the hill.

And he ought to take the kids something—candy, soda pop. Or ice cream. It wouldn't hurt to sweeten Pearlean up a little. Through the glass front of the A&P he could see folks jam-packed and laying hold of groceries like everything was free. The commotion drew him in.

He heard one of the cashiers yell, "We all out of bread!" As he started down the aisle he saw that the milk and egg refrigerators were empty too. The checkout line extended nearly to the rear of the store.

It didn't matter that the river made no direct threat to their end of the city, people in Rattlebone took all natural disasters—wherever they happened—as personal warnings. *There, but for the grace of God, go I.* They fortified themselves with meat and canned goods. James thought he'd be better off stopping at Doll's Market where he wouldn't have to stand in line.

There too, as he pushed through the swinging door, he heard Doll's husky voice announcing, "No bread, no lunch ham, and no more candles!" to the twenty-odd customers waiting to pay for their groceries. Soda pop and candy were no big thing, but he felt like killing more time before going home to deal with Pearlean. He spotted Thomas Pemberton in the line—Old Uncle he called him—and waved.

"Shorty—boy, what you doin down here?" Thomas called to him.

"Just messin 'round, fixin to go home," James said, noting the weariness in his own voice. Thomas motioned for him to come closer.

"I guess you heard about the levee and all," Thomas said. Before James could answer, Thomas gave up his place in line and launched into his account of the record-breaking water levels the river had reached, all the little towns and whistle stops it had washed away in the past four days, including hollows and creek bridges he had known as a boy. Finally he gave James the latest news, that the Civil Defense was calling for volunteers to sandbag the levee on the south side of the city.

"They ain't payin, but they sayin that they need a lot of people," Thomas told him. "Soon as Wes closes the barbershop, me and him are thinkin 'bout goin out there to see what's what."

It had its appeal. Still, James said, "I guess I'll head on in. Pearl'll be wondering where I am." He told Thomas to "say hi to Miss Lydia," and fished around in the bin of penny candies.

It felt good to be out rushing around in the streets. This desire to be unfettered in the world came down on him sometimes like rain on an arid field. He drank it in, imagining the streets of Chicago or Harlem, places he had never seen. He pictured the wide ocean he had crossed to New Guinea during the war. Whenever he felt this way, he let the imaginings swell, and when they reached the point of forming themselves into ideas, he turned them loose, let them fly to be recaptured at any time he chose.

If he hadn't had to sell the truck, he could drive out to Armourdale just to see the river at the levee. Since he had moved back home, Pearl watched him like a hawk, he couldn't take a single breath on his own. All of what he knew to be her anger, and all of what he guessed was her hope, had crystallized in the single thing she must have repeated to him every day. Whether it was about his money, his time, or his attitude in general, she kept it constantly in his face.

"I have to come first in your life, James. Me and the kids, we have to come first."

She was justified, he couldn't argue. In her eyes he had up and left her for October Brown, and when he had gotten himself in way over his head and had to sell his truck, only then did he crawl back home. It would be a long, long time before Pearl would get over it.

He turned down Seventh Street toward Wes's Barber Shop. A six-bottle carton of Nehi's and a handful of Tootsie Rolls weren't going to cut him any slack tonight, either, when Pearlean found out about the Cordon job.

He crossed over to the Texaco station. Maybe it would be better for them both if he took his time getting home. He dropped a dime in the slot. He would call and tell her he'd be late. But why have a big blowout? Maybe for once he could take the time to clear his head, figure out what he needed to say to get her to understand him. He hung up the receiver and retrieved his dime.

When he got to the barbershop, Thomas was there waiting for Wes to lock up.

"You mean Pearlean's gonna let you go out to the river tonight?" Thomas said and winked at Wes.

If anyone else had said it, James might have bristled, but this was Thomas. Thomas Pemberton wasn't kin, and he wasn't James's ace-boon-coon, but James knew that despite the difference in their ages, Thomas would always be in his corner. He could count on Thomas to loan him money, and Thomas even gave him odd jobs in the pretense of letting him earn it. Of course he stayed on his back about going to church and saving for a house he could buy for Pearl and the kids. But that came with the territory.

"So you goin out there with us?" Wes asked him.

"What does it look like?" James said.

"Aw, so now, all of a sudden, you the man," Wes joked. "I saw you callin up to get permission."

And Thomas put in, "Don't you be gettin me on the outs with Pearlean. Next thing you know, Lydia'll be getting on my case 'cause Pearlean is upset about your foolishness. I ain't said you can ride in my truck yet," he said, but he was grinning.

As the sun gradually sank, they climbed into the cab of Thomas's truck and crept with the traffic out Seventh Street toward the bridge. At the wheel Thomas hummed a piece of a hymn. Wes hung his arm out the other window and sucked on one Lucky Strike after another. James wedged his shoulders between the two of them and distracted himself with memories. October Brown. His schoolteacher woman. His chocolate-covered cherry. The way she would walk with him into the semidarkness of Shady Maurice's after-hours place. "*Chez de*," she told him every time. "It's *Chez de* Maurice, not *Shady*."

He could see himself smile as he looked into her face. She had a way of hooking her arm through his, touching his shoulder, leaning in for him to plant his kiss on the pink-white spot of her cheek. Always, then, her sweet muskiness would blind him.

UP AHEAD, TAILLIGHTS red-studded the road. Wes leaned farther out the window to get a clearer view. Thomas concentrated on the stop-and-start of the cars in front of him. By the time they caught sight of the bridge, night and river had come full into bloom.

It begins sometime in late September. The snows of Montana, Iowa, Minnesota sift down, layer after layer, undisturbed except in streets of cities like Bismarck and Dubuque. All over the plains the snows go on falling through November, Christmas, the dull of February. In March, when the earth changes its angle and thaws, the Kaw and Missouri join the fluid rampage down the Mississippi's grand troughway to the Gulf of Mexico. And if the Mississippi swells beyond the pores of its ample bed, every river, every creek, brook, and pond up through the Midwest to the Canadian line confirms the law that water seeks its own level.

James was restless. The force of the river and the excited air above it captivated him as he looked out from the cab of Thomas's truck into the deceptive sheen on the black water.

At the other side of the bridge a highway patrolman waved them out of the line of cars and onto a hastily made gravel road through overgrowth and marshes. After a while James saw a series of floodlights and heard the hum of the generator punctuated by the "Over here!" shouts of men.

They followed the gravel road to the work site made brighter than daylight by the floodlights strung makeshift to a tree. The men looked flat, unreal. The colors of their shirts and overalls were bleached in the bright light, and sharp shadows danced around them. The entire area was a theater enveloped by featureless dark. The trooper who directed the activity at the solid mountain of sandbags explained that they should move quickly to load Thomas's truck with bags. Then, following the gravel and the lights, haul them "up the line," closer to the river.

"One vehicle at a time," the trooper said. "The road is narrow. We can't have nobody getting out into the marshes."

After a whole day of sitting James was primed for action. Judging from the slow ride out to the levee, it was probably after nine. Pearlean and the kids would have gone on and had supper by now.

Once when his daughter had surprised him at the supper table and asked him about his stay away from home, he had managed to say some tired something about people needing time. But that wasn't it, not really. October Brown? Well she was something else again. Sure, he wanted her. A man would have to be a fool not to want her. But more and more it wasn't about her or any other woman. Whatever it was that had kept him in that rented room for a year had something to do with the satisfaction he got from following his mind out to the rising river on a dark night when all of Rattlebone, all of Kansas City, huddled in their houses.

And suppose he wanted to see the coast, say, and decided to take a trip alone, or even with Pearl? He hadn't come to that bridge yet, and when he did, he would cross it. Although they had never talked about leaving Kansas City, he could imagine Pearlean saying, "Name one thing they got in California that we can't get here."

The men had loaded up the truck and had driven so close that James could hear water rushing. He and Thomas let down the tailgate and lifted sandbags into pairs of hands. James worked up a sweat. He watched the double line of long shadows swing sand pillows from one set of hands to the next. These men were probably scared, or at least nervous. But if he didn't know better, he would think he was at any one of a hundred construction sites he'd seen. The artificial light, the generator noise, men hauling sand—none of this looked dangerous. If he was going to get any sympathy from Pearl, he was going to have to exaggerate a few of the details.

"They're sayin they closed the bridge down soon as we come off it," Thomas said. "Guess they got to be careful. Who knows, the bridge could go too."

When they emptied and refilled the truck with bags next time, James thought he might walk up closer to the river, see what there was to see, maybe sandbag on the actual levee for a while. On the white gravel, he followed the line of men until he could hear the river roaring over the generator's hum. Just ahead, the levee—a hill of sandbags now—rose ten or twelve feet. Men had stationed themselves like steps to toss the bags on the topmost layer. A trooper paced the ground at the base and kept constant dialogue with the crackle from his walkie-talkie.

"What's the word?" James asked the trooper.

"Don't know much yet," he said. "We got men strung out for two miles, and the river is supposed to crest here in another couple of hours. The Civil Defense will tell us when the time comes to pull out. Unless they do, we'll probably be here all night and we better hope it don't start raining."

James climbed up a few feet. This was better. Right on the other side of this wall the torrent of water rushed past. He could feel it when he stood stock-still, the rumble, the pull.

"They evacuated Lenexa earlier, you know," one of the men said. He swung a sandbag into James's hands. "Good thing, too. The trooper said it's gone under."

"I guess Bonner Springs is next," James said. He passed one bag and readied his hands for the next.

"Yeah, some parts of it," the man said, and slung the bag of sand into James's hands. "I've got family waiting," he said. "I'm thinking about pulling out before too long."

The man had said it with such a note of delight that James wanted to see his face. When the man turned again, his expression revealed little. Within the next hour, groups of men came and went. Then as midnight approached, a commotion broke out in the direction of the bridge—James thought he saw the flash of a red light against the dark.

Soon the sound of revving engines faded in. Then a loudspeaker boomed: "Evacuate the area! Evacuate! All personnel leave this area!"

The voice said something else about Shawnee Mission and the bridge, but James couldn't hear it for the noise of the gravel stampede. Men leapt from their perches on the sandbags and ran toward the generator-light. As James scrambled to get his footing, the light went out. A collective cry issued from the men.

James struggled to keep his footing. He thought if he could just head straight for the generator where the light had been, he would find his way out of there. But blinding darkness disoriented him. Straight ahead from here, he thought, but, then, hadn't he seen trees between the levee and the generator? Stay on the gravel, he thought, but already there seemed to be no gravel under his feet, or was there?

"The levee is out! Run!" somebody shouted.

With his eyes open to pitch black, he groped the air in front of his face like a sleepwalker and ran in the direction of the car engines. But they too had moved farther away. He heard the footfalls of men far ahead of him. He closed his eyes to gain balance, and ran faster.

Just run, he told himself. Don't try to see. A crashing sound, a tree falling? Were men laughing or crying? Surely the river wasn't taking them already. Making time now, he's making time. Don't try to see. Run. His heart rumbled in his chest, his ankle buckled. Was that gravel under his feet? Keep your balance, run straight. Behind him a roaring like a train. Faster. Pressure in his eyes, in his ears. Like a train churning up trees! His chest burned. He can run faster than this. His arms pumped. Water! His legs. Water! His hands. Mud! Men thrashed around him. All of them lost! No air! His nose, his chest exploded. Got to hold on. Swim. Got to.

His head went light. After what seemed like ages, he came to. At his own door. Pearl opens it. "We waited," she says. She leads him to the supper table and they sit down with Irene and Junie and her sister's children. She makes them all hold hands while she says the blessing. She sounds young, like a girl, like when he first met her. She finishes grace with "Good bread, good meat, good Lord, let's eat!" and they all laugh freely. She watches them eat, sprinkles more sugar on Junie's rice, and when Irene runs her bread around her plate for the last drop of gravy, Pearl pulls bits of meat from the neckbone on her plate and gives them to her daughter. "Eat up. You've got ten more years to grow." Her hands are quick. *What?* her eyes say when she sees him watching. *Who me?* they say. She tests his thoughts with a smile.

A SHARP PAIN shot through his shoulder. His arm.

"Open up your eyes, fool! Shorty! Stand up! Open your eyes!"

James coughed and gagged on water and river slime. Thomas and Wes held him up, pounded his back. The three of them stood thigh-deep in marsh water.

"You all right, Shorty?" Wes said. "You almost drowned yourself hollering like something got a hold of you."

James nodded his head yes. When he wiped away some of the mud, he could make out only dark and darker, then forms—sky, trees, pale gravel. The river's rumble oriented him, and he shook the two men off.

"They're sayin the river is crestin. No need to take no chances. Let's get on home," Thomas said.

They joined other men on the gravel path to Thomas's truck and began the slow drive out. James thought he must have looked some kind of crazy, like a scared kid wallowing around, drowning his own fool self in the marshes. He was grateful that no one spoke. Once he could see the lights from the Seventh Street bridge he could not bear to be closed in.

"Let me out, Thomas, I'll walk the rest of the way."

"You can't walk, Shorty. You a mess and they ain't lettin nobody use the bridge. We got to go clean 'cross the state line through Missouri to get home," Thomas said, but he pulled over.

"You sure you all right? What you want us to tell Pearlean? You know she's gonna be lookin for you."

"Don't tell her nothin," James said.

Maybe by nearly drowning him in the marshes, God was telling him something. That this one life was the only life he would ever have. Maybe he should simply walk away. The gulf between the kind of life he sometimes imagined and his life with Pearl seemed as uncrossable as a wild river.

That night, furious though it was, the Kaw swept away many a sandbag but kept within its banks. All night James walked —out through Armourdale, across the Missouri line, past houses filled with people who waited in the dark for someone to return to them, then back across to Kansas and the hill above the natural collision of two rivers—in a roundabout circle home.

CHERRY

BOMB

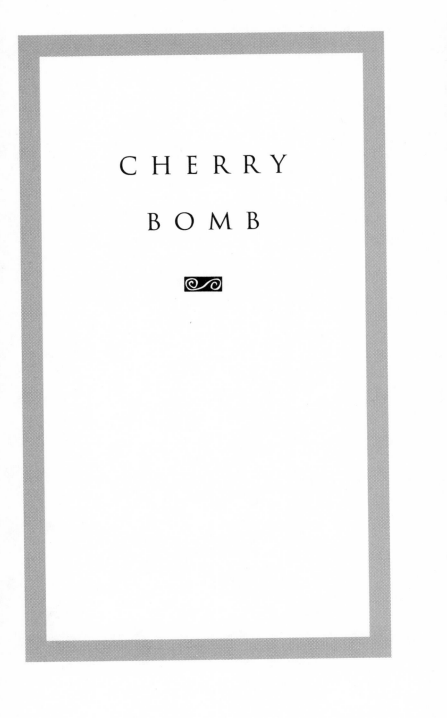

I T WAS TWO summers before I would put my thin-penny bus token in the slot and ride the Fifth Street trolley all the way to the end of the line to junior high. Life was measured in summers then, and the expression "I am in this world, but not of it" appealed to me. I wasn't sure what it meant, but it had just the right ring for a lofty statement I should adopt. That Midwest summer broke records for straight over-one-hundred-degree days in July, and Mr. Calhoun still came around with that-old-thing of an ice truck. Our mother still bought a help-him-out block of ice to leave in the backyard for us to lick or sit on. It was the summer that the Bible's plague of locusts came. Evening sighed its own relief in a locust hum that swelled from the cattails next to the cemetery, from the bridal wreath shrubs and the pickle grass that my younger cousin, Bea, combed and braided on our side of the alley.

I kept a cherry bomb and a locked diary in the closet under the back steps where Bea, restrained by my suggestion that the Hairy Man hid there, wouldn't try to find them. It was an established, Daddy-said-so fact that at night the Hairy Man went anywhere he wanted to go but in the daytime he stayed inside the yellow house on Sherman Avenue near our school. During the school year if we were so late that the patrol boys had gone inside, we would see him in his fenced-in yard, wooly-headed and bearded, hollering things we dared not repeat until a nurse kind of woman in a bandanna came out and took him back inside the house with the windows painted light blue, which my mother said was a peaceful color for somebody shell-shocked.

If you parted the heavy coats between the raggedy mouton that once belonged to my father's mother, who, my father said, was his Heart when she died, and the putrid-colored jacket my father wore when he got shipped out to the dot in the Pacific Ocean where, he said, the women wore one piece of cloth and looked as fine as wine in the summertime, you would find yourself right in the middle of our cave-dark closet. Then, if you closed your eyes, held your hands up over your head, placed one foot in front of the other, walked until the tips of your fingers touched the smooth cool of slanted plaster all the way down to where you had to slue your feet and walk squat-legged, fell to your knees and felt around on the floor —then you would hit the strong-smelling cigar box. My box of private things.

From time to time my cousins Bea and Eddy stayed with us, and on the Fourth of July the year before, Eddy had lit a cherry bomb in a Libby's corn can and tried to lob it over the house into the alley. Before it reached the top of the porch it went off, and a piece of tin shot God-is-whipping-you straight for Eddy's eye. By the time school started that year, Eddy had a keloid like a piece of twine down the side of his face and a black patch he had to wear until he got his glass eye that stared in a fixed angle at the sky. Nick, Eddy's friend, began calling Eddy "Black-Eyed Pea."

After Eddy's accident, he gave me a cherry bomb. His last. I kept it in my cigar box as a sort of memento of good times. Even if I had wanted to explode it, my mother had threatened to do worse to us if we so much as looked at fireworks again. Except for Christmas presents, it was the first thing anybody ever gave me.

But my diary was my most private thing, except for the other kind of private thing, which Eddy's friend Nick was always telling me he was going to put his hand up my dress and feel someday when I stopped being babyish about it. I told that to my diary right along with telling the other Nick-smells-like-Dixie-Peach things I wrote every afternoon, sitting in my room with the bed that Bea and I shared pulled up against the door. I always wrote until it was time for my father to come home and take off his crusty brogans that sent little rocks of dried cement flying.

One evening after supper, I sat on the curb with Bea and Wanda calling out cars the way my father sometimes did with us from the glider on our front porch. The engine sounds, the sleekness of shapes, the intricacies of chrome in the grillwork were on his list of what he would get when his ship came in. Buick Dynaflow! Fifty-three Ford! Bea kept rock-chalk score on the curb until Nick rode up on his dump-parts bike. Situated precariously on the handlebars, he pedaled backwards, one of his easy postures. He rode his bike in every possible pose, including his favorite invention, the J.C., which had him sailing along, standing upright on the seat with his arms out in mock crucifixion.

"You wanna ride?"

Of course I wanted to, but Nick was stingy when it came to his bike, and I knew he was teasing.

"It's gettin dark, but I'll ride you up to the highway and back if you want to," he said. He sounded like he meant it.

"Okay, but no fooling around," I said, and at once I was on the seat behind him, close up to his Dixie Peach hair. Pumping up and over two long hills, we rode a mile in the twilight. Later with our knees drawn up, we sat to rest on the soft bluff overlooking the yellow-stippled asphalt road, calling out cars. Beyond the highway toward the river, I could see the horizon's last flames. The faint smell of bacon rode sweetly on the breeze from the packing house upshore.

"Star light, star bright, the first star I see tonight, I wish I may, I wish I might . . ."

At first Nick wouldn't look up. "I don't see no star," he said.

I pointed. "See right up there, it's the North Star."

"How you know?"

"My mother showed it to me."

Then he looked. "Bet that ain't it."

"Bet it is. When it gets all the way dark, it'll be on the handle of the Little Dipper."

"If it's on the handle by the time the nine o'clock whistle blows, you get to ride my bike tomorrow all day. If it ain't, I get a kiss."

"Uh-uh, Nick," I said. "Let's just bet a hot pickle."

"Okay, Mamma's-Baby, okay, Miss Can't-Get-No-Brassiere, Miss Bow-Legs," and he rubbed my leg.

"Quit!" I said, and brushed his hand away. He did it again and I knocked his hand away again.

"Bet nobody ever touched your pussy."

"Ain't nobody ever going to, either."

"See if I don't," and he pushed me backwards, stuck his salty tongue in my mouth. His groping fingers up the leg of my shorts scratched when he pulled at my underpants. Then, like an arrow, fast and straight, his finger shot pain inside me. I punched him hard and he—"Ow, girl!"—stopped. I jumped up—"I'm telling"—and ran. He grabbed my ankle. His "Don't tell," then his "You better not" filled the air around me. But my own steely "I ain't scared" walked me all the way home. Halfway there I heard the pad of bike tires behind me on the brick street, and Nick sailed by, standing on the seat, his arms out in a J.C.

"Girl, I sent Eddy out looking for you, where you been?" my mother asked.

"I was up by Janice's house," I told her.

That night the tinge of pink in my underpants said that I should put epsom salts in the bathtub and hope that nothing bad had happened down there. When my mother asked me what I was doing with epsom salts, I told her, "Chiggers."

But I spelled it all out to my diary in I-am-in-this-world language. Nick: his shiny black-walnut skin, the soft fragrance of Dixie Peach in his hair, the cutoff overalls he wore with only one shoulder strap fastened so that I had to hold on to his bare shoulders even though they were sweaty. And in but-not-of-this-world language I told my diary the wish I had for him to get some kind of home training, go to church, act right, and not want to feel in my panties, and the soft kiss I wanted him to learn. I also told my diary how Eddy was pretending to be able to see with his glass eye, but how I heard him crying at night because he wanted to go with Wanda Coles and she made a fool out of him by having him watch her hand move back and forth in front of his face.

The next morning, when I gave my father his lunch box and his ice-water thermos and held the screen door for him, I saw Nick leaning and looking to be noticed in the Y of his apricot tree across the alley that was the boundary between our backyards. It was washday, a good opportunity for me to ignore him.

"Four loads before the sun gets hot," my mother said, and we rolled the washer off the back porch and into the middle of the kitchen, with two rinse tubs set side by side on my father's workbench. I stripped the beds still full of Bea and Eddy and the tobacco smell of my father and soft scent of my mother's Pond's cream. Underneath the mattress in their bedroom I always saw the same envelope of old war bonds, the small book of old ration stamps. And this time I found a magazine, *True Romance*, and inside it a card with roses on the front and a my-love-grows message, unsigned. At first I thought it must be from my father to my mother or vice versa. But as I ran to the kitchen with my discovery, I suddenly thought of my *private* cigar box, and slowly I went back up the stairs to sort out the knot of bedclothes on the floor.

Nick waited until the last sheet was stretched and pinned and the long pole was jacked up to raise the clothesline higher before he said a word.

"Found a new pedal for my bike," he yelled. I went inside the screen door but turned to see him sliding down from his perch.

"You can ride all day," he said through the screen. "Aw, hi, Miss Wilson."

"What you doing running around this early?" my mother asked him. "I know your mamma left something for you to get done 'fore she gets home," she said. "I bet you haven't even washed your face yet."

"I already did everything," Nick lied. The naps on his head were still separate.

"Then you can get your friend Eddy out the bed, and y'all can go to the store for me. We need some more starch."

It tickled Nick that he had gained entrance to the goings-on of our house, and he raced up the back stairs calling out, "Hey, Eddy, let's go!" I was hanging up line number two when they jostled down the unpaved alleyway, picking up rocks and throwing them at birds. "Come on, girl," my mother called. "We got a mess of overalls in here."

On washdays, when my mother said "Catch as catch can," we revelled in the break of routine, eating whatever we could find raw in a bowl for breakfast—and whatever we could get between two slices of bread for lunch. That noon, in my mother's got-to-get-this-done expression, I tried to find the secret that must have brought her the card of roses. Suppose Nick gave me such a card. But I could not picture my mother looking at the man holding the woman on the front of *True Romance*. I made mustard-and-onion-sandwiches for me and Bea and wandered among the clotheslines, waiting for Nick to ride by so I could ignore him some more.

When the sun was at its highest point, Eddy and Nick came into the kitchen for a cool drink of water. Nick grinned at me through Eddy's entire speech to my mother about how hot it was, how the Missouri River had backed up enough from recent rains to fill the hole that wasn't even stagnant this summer, how the still water was so clear you could see the tadpoles, and how my father had said even *he* used to swim over there.

As Eddy went on, Nick said I could go swimming with them if I wanted to. I couldn't swim, and I knew that he knew it, which made his asking sweet.

"I saw the Dipper last night," he said. "You can ride my bike tomorrow since y'all have to wash today."

"I don't want to ride your bike," I said. "You don't know how to act. Besides, my father is building me one for myself, and it's going to be a girl's bike."

"You can't *make* a girl's bike," Nick said. "They don't throw away those kind of frames at the dump."

"Okay," my mother said to them. "Y'all can go. But Nick, you watch out for Eddy. He can't see as good as you can, so don't be cuttin the fool in the water. Y'all be back here 'fore supper, you hear?"

Nick winked at me. Rolling my eyes had become my best response. Undaunted, he pushed Eddy toward the screen door, and by the time it slammed, they were on Nick's bike, headed for the Missouri River hole.

MY BEST FRIEND, Cece, lived with her grandmother over the summer, too far away from our house. And so I hung around with Wanda most of the time, though I usually told her none of my secrets. Really, the only thing I had against Wanda was her long, straight hair in bangs and two braids that she made even longer with colored plastic clothespins clamped onto the ends.

"Can you come out?" she asked through the screen.

"Sprinkle the shirts and ball them up, and you can go," my mother said. I filled the ironing basket with sprinkled clothes and left with Wanda. Out under our crabapple tree we sat rubbing chunks of ice over our legs and arms in the still afternoon.

"I came to tell you something," Wanda said.

"What?"

"Guess," she said.

"I don't know."

"It has something to do with this," she said, and reached into the elastic band of her shorts. She struggled with the size of the thing until it cleared her pocket and she held it up. "See."

It was a small, thick diary, a tan color, with letters that read FIVE YEAR DIARY in gold on the cover, and when she felt around in her pocket, a small key—all just like mine. Then deftly she unlocked the lock.

"Read this," she said. I took the book from her and confirmed that each page held a lined section for each day of five years. It was enough to see that Wanda, who wasn't even my friend, had managed to secure for herself the same precious thing I had done Miss Gray's chores for. Because Miss Gray next door was grossly overweight and couldn't get her arms up, I had oiled and braided her thick, sticky hair. I had swept her house, rugs and all. Since she couldn't get around very well, I had run to the store to get her messy tobacco, and got the boneless ham too that she said she ought to cut back on—all in order to collect two dollars' worth of dimes in a sock for the journal that would record the most vital facts about five years of my life.

That was enough without Wanda insisting that I read it.

"I can't read your writing," I said.

She took the book from my hands. "It says, 'Today I became

a woman. I didn't get the cramps like everyone said I would. Now I can wear heels and red-fox stockings, and know that I have put away all the childish things I used to do. I am truly happy.' You know what that means?" she asked me.

"Yeah, that's nice," was all I could muster.

"I think every girl should have a diary, because it happens to every girl and it's a day you should always remember. You ought to get one."

"Yeah," I said.

By the time my father got home, I had done my two-faced best to convince Wanda that she would look like Lena Horne if she just wore kit curlers to bed. All the while I delighted in the way her bangs fell like a stringy rag mop in her eyes that day.

By suppertime I was sick of Wanda and happy to go looking for Eddy and Nick at the river. My mother insisted Wanda should keep me company, and so off we went, hopscotching our way on the bricks until we came to the new concrete sidewalk with cracks to avoid in the name of good luck. Down the soft slope above the highway we scooted, and when the whiz of cars broke, we flew across the highway and ran down the muddy hollow to the plain of wild onion, garlic, asparagus, and no telling what kinds of snakes to the place where the stand of short trees leaned, and the noisy rush of cars gave way to the noisy rush of river to come.

There on the ground just through the trees, Eddy lay on his back with his arms careless at his sides. Something wavelike through me made the hairs stand up on my arms, and I took off running to him. I stood above him just long enough to see his blind eye staring before he jumped awake, opening his other eye. In that instant I realized that not since the cherry-bomb accident had I seen Eddy asleep, and therefore did not know that he slept with the eye open.

"What are you doing laying here like this? Where's Nick?"

"I got too tired and Nick didn't want to come out yet," Eddy said, and he got up, pulled on his undershirt, and picked up Nick's bike at his side.

Wanda and I went to the bank of the cloudy green pool and called for Nick to come out. We called again and again. "Nick! Nick! We're going to leave you here and take your bike!"

"Nick!" Eddy called from across the water. "Nick!" Eddy called again and it went through the hairs on my arms. Wanda and I couldn't hold back our "Nick! Come on!" We looked into the pool but saw nothing through the muddy green.

We ran around the pool to Eddy's side.

"You don't think he went on over to the river, do you?"

"Not without telling me," Eddy said.

"Then where is he? Where was he when you came out?"

"He was right there." Eddy pointed. "Right out there in the middle. He can swim better than anybody. Let's just wait, hear?"

"Uh-uh," Wanda said. "We ought to get somebody. Suppose something happened to him."

I hated Wanda more than anybody and anything. "Let's just wait," I echoed Eddy.

"I'm going," Wanda said. As she ran, she yelled, "I'm going to get y'all's daddy. My mamma's going to be mad. I ain't got no business by the river."

"Nick's gonna get it. Nick's gonna get it," Eddy kept repeating as we stood looking toward the river, hoping to see Nick's white-toothed, nappy-headed self come bopping through the short trees, looking for his bike to go off on while we walked home, probably meeting my father on the way, probably telling him never mind, and most likely rolling our eyes at Wanda, who always acts like she knows so much.

Nick's gonna get it. When I get my girl's bike I'm not letting him touch it unless he swears he will not show off like it's some piece of junk he doesn't have to treat right. Unless he says we can ride together up to the highway and he says he's sorry for not acting right. I am in this world, but not of it. I am in this world.

Eddy and I waited, watched the pool turn deeper green, and the sun slant light like fire through the trees.

First came my father, the sweat on his face and head shining, his arms wagging out at his sides as he sloshed through the tall grass toward us. Then Mamma behind him in her flower-print wash dress, calling us like she couldn't see we were standing right there. Then, really bad, Nick's mother with her gray and crimson elevator operator's uniform still on from work, running in high-heel shoes, calling Nick. Then Bea with Wanda and Mrs. Coles holding Puddin's hand, walking fast, then standing still outside the realm of confusion. Then the questions and Nick's mother shaking Eddy and my mother snatching her away from us and my father jumping in with his overalls on and Nick's mother crying and my mother saying, "Hush, now, it's gonna be all right," and Eddy closing his good eye tight and me saying the Lord's Prayer for us all. Then my father spitting out water and hollering and going down again and up again and hollering, "Get them kids away from here, get 'em away!" and Wanda and her mother running toward the highway, and my mother making us go stand over by the trees and Nick's mother pulling away from Mamma like she was going to jump into the water herself.

When my father laid Nick's body on the grass, I could see that Nick's hands were curled like they could never be straightened. Mamma walked his mother over to him and they held those curled-up hands until the ambulance people came and covered up his face. Nick's mother and Mamma went with them. Wanda's mother took me and Eddy and my father and Bea home in their Dynaflow.

That night Mamma held her waist and cried a lot. Eddy put his bed up to his door so that nobody could go in. My father said that I could stay up as long as I wanted and he sat out on the porch with his cigarettes. I could hear the glider creak every now and then, and I knew he was dozing and waking in the dark. Bea was so quiet in our room, she was almost not there. I sat awake in our bed for what seemed like the longest time, as if I had been sentenced to wait for something that could never come. I didn't feel at all like I would cry. Blank was what I felt, blank and swollen tight.

Groping my way, I parted the coats between the mouton and my father's rough wool, stretched my arms, and walked my hands down the ceiling to the box. Although I could not yet bring myself to throw away a month of my recorded life, my diary would not be useful, I had nothing to write. I found the cherry bomb. In the kitchen, I took the box of matches from the shelf over the stove and crept out the screen door. The glider creaked, but I stole out of the yard across the alley, through Nick's yard, out to the sidewalk and on.

From the soft bluff, I could hear the rush of the river above the hum of locusts. A fingernail sliver of moon laid out the highway gray and bent. The Little Dipper tilted. I struck a match and lit the green stem. When it sizzled, I threw it high and far, exploding the whole summer.

THE
ROOMERS

I TELL PEMBERTON all the time, some people just don't believe fat meat's greasy. Them's the kind of people you have to watch, let them know you mean business, or they walk on you like they walking on a cement sidewalk. Me and Pemberton done run this house a long time. We bought it at the beginning of the war, when everybody and his brother was going or coming, dying or buying, one or the other. We was supposed to be starting us a family and when that didn't work out, me and Pemberton thought we'd just as well to rent the house out. Near about every year we fixed on it, put nice furniture in all the rooms, decent rugs on the floors. We take in mostly teachers because they don't keep up no noise, most of them, and they tend to their own business. That way you don't get riffraff.

This whole thing started when we give the kitchenette to a teacher named October Brown. I don't suspect Pemberton took to her when she first come in here. The chile was a little too much on the dark side for him to get excited about. Not that he would have turned down her money, he's black himself. Light skin may be upper-crust to him, but it don't mean nothin in my book. Let me tell you, I have known Thomas Pemberton to look twice at more than one high-yellow woman with good hair, and years ago, it near about cost him everything we had. But like I said, this thing with October Brown wasn't about how she looked. She wasn't nowhere near light skin, head hadn't been close to no straightening comb, either, wooly as a sheep's behind. Pitiful how young they start them teaching. She couldn't have been no more than twenty-one or two. "May I see Mr. Pemberton?" she asked us.

I tell him all the time about answering the door with no clothes on. Don't no well-to-do people answer the door in their undershirt and house shoes.

"Who're you?" Pemberton asked her. She told him who she was.

"I was told you might have a room to rent," she said.

"Depends," I said over Pemberton's shoulder. He would've stood there all day hemmin and hawin.

She'd done been down at the teachers' college two years and finished up at the university. They'd just hired her on up here in Rattlebone to teach the third grade at Stowe. She said her people were from down south somewhere, I done forgot where, but said she was raised in Ohio. Talked real proper. Pemberton liked proper talkers.

"We might have something," I said. "Come on, I'll show you the place." I sent Pemberton on back to his newspaper.

Long time ago, fact, soon as we got our first place, Pemberton wanted to take in roomers. No indeedy, I said. True, Pemberton was at the packing house then, working nights, but I didn't want nobody living with us right away.

Them wasn't no good times for us. We hadn't done been married a year when I up and got pregnant. Pemberton is the living proof that some men act a fool when their wife is carrying a child. I don't know if Pemberton just didn't know what to do with himself or what, but he started running around with a woman that lived a block over from us. Mamie Turner. High-yellow woman with the long hair and what I call a large following, you know, big hips. I never knew much about the woman except she had some children already, didn't have no man, and she was sure Pemberton was going to belong to her. Oh, she had a nerve. Come walking by any time of day she felt like it. Walked real slow in front of the house, looking. Never once spoke, not even a nod at me, unless Pemberton was home.

What kind of a fool did they think I was? I might have been heavy and clumsy, but I wasn't blind and crippled. I decided to see for myself what was what, and walked around to where the woman lived one day, strolled right up and knocked on her door. Don't you know Pemberton himself opened the door just like he lived there. You could have bought him for a penny. But did that stop him? No indeedy, he acted like he couldn't get enough of her.

Well. I'd done had enough of both of them. I took and set all Pemberton's clothes out by the trash for the ragman. Took his suits, his shirts, his shoes, everything. Put them in gunnysacks and set them right at the alley. He didn't know they was out there. That day he come home from work or wherever, and I told him just to go ahead on. If he wanted Mamie Turner so bad he had to sneak around with her while I was big with his baby, just go ahead on.

Oh, it was a mess. Needless to say, Pemberton got himself and his clothes together and crawled on back with me. He paid the price though. Reckon we both did. A couple of weeks later when the baby come here dead and no bigger than my hand, he blamed himself. Guess he felt like God was punishing him. Them was hard times for us.

I never heard what become of Mamie Turner. People talked. Said one of her boys belonged to Pemberton. He never said one way or the other, said just let it be. One thing for sure, he knew better than to bring some bastard child of that woman's in my face.

Later on, when we got this place and started to take in roomers, we made it clear that if you lived under our roof, wasn't going to be no foolishness. Professional people know the stakes, and we never allowed no one in here who wasn't decent. We done had preachers, railroad men, plus we had a few city workers come down from Topeka, mailmen and what not. After while, though, we said nothing but teachers.

"We don't have but two vacancies, but you can see the whole place, all five rooms," I told October Brown. Don't hurt for a new girl to see how the old ones keep theirs up. Right away she liked the kitchenette.

"Where you staying now?" I asked her.

"I'm over at Reverend Jackson's in a double room," she said.

Reverend was a man of God, but from what I had heard, his place was high and wasn't too clean.

I told her, "I suspect me and Pemberton'll make up our minds and call over there directly."

So we did. We give October Brown the kitchenette. Teachers always saving up because they ain't got nothing to spend their money on unless they sending it home. Sure enough, October Brown said she would pay whatever we was charging.

"Generally our roomers get breakfast and supper," I told

her. "Since you got the kitchenette your meals is extra. Saturdays y'all have to make do, or do without," I told her. And I give her all the rules about no smoking, no drinking, and no men. "You can see any men friends you want in the front room, but they can't go upstairs. This ain't that kind of house."

That was all right by her. Said she didn't have no men friends. Said she could get her own breakfast, which she must did, but I never smelled nothing coming out that kitchenette in the morning.

The day she moved in I had a Ruth Circle meeting at church. Pemberton and me ate early and I decided I'd fix a quick little supper for the roomers and set it out. Little buffet. Down she come and looked at the table.

"Help yourself to whatever you want," I said. I introduced her around the table so nobody could say I didn't see to it that they knew who she was. Jocelyn Jones was at Stowe too. Mary Esther and tall, skinny Albertine Scott was at Attucks. Old Miss Dumas had done retired years ago, but she kept up with what was going on. October Brown sat down, and when they passed around the food, she put one spoonful of slaw on her plate. Nothing else. One spoonful of slaw.

"You ain't hungry?" Pemberton asked her.

Oh, she don't care for no conies and beans, Mr. Pemberton, she says, talking proper. But, she says, she'll just have a little bread and butter too and be fine.

I could feel my mouth wanting to say something, but I didn't. When I was leaving out the house, I could hear the rest of them commence to sighing and fussing over what we was and what we wasn't having for supper. Pemberton wasn't no better. He likes to eat with the girls, carrying on about first one thing, then the other. They go on about coloreds and whites, about the school situation, the whites got this and that, and we ain't. If it was left to Pemberton, I'd be fixing pies and cakes every day just so they could sit at the table and chew the cud longer.

Hadn't a month passed when a certain young man come sniffing around. Mr. Carter was good at fixing things and he used to help out Pemberton. Every year the two of them hung the storm windows up, but this particular day Carter was sick or something and sent over this boy he knew named James. They called him Shorty. James "Shorty" Wilson. Nice look-ing, about twenty-six or seven. Slick jitterbug. I don't know what went on between him and her, but I do know that James Shorty Boy got down off the ladder, come inside the house, and went up to October Brown's room, just as big. I had a fit. I told Pemberton he better get that boy out of there.

Well, Pemberton got him out. "We can't have no men upstairs. Now you git to gittin," Pemberton told him. "These is schoolteachers here," he said.

Shorty said, "Shoot, I didn't know that." Said his screw-driver was between the windows in one of the rooms and he just come in to get it in the kitchenette. But it got so every now and then, mostly now, he come by and sat right on the divan in the front room, talking to her.

Me and Pemberton didn't keep the place like a convent for the nuns, but we was on the good-house list for the school board all them years because we knew what they wanted for their teachers. Naturally if they lived with us, they walked the line. Pemberton always thought the girls would just catch on and do right. Not me. I don't know of no tale big.enough to outdo what some of them teachers done tried one time or other. Truth was, most of them was careful. That chile Oc-

tober Brown, though, she wasn't no more careful than the
sun is careful about coming up.

After while, I guess talking wasn't good enough for her and
the fellow. Reverend's wife, Johnnie Mae, called up over here
one day about some story she got from one of the women in
her choir. The way she told it, she had seen October Brown
with Shorty at Shady Maurice's joint out in the county. Said
she was all over him, right out in the public. I wanted to ask
Johnnie Mae what the woman was doing out there herself.

Pemberton walked around here talking about "Now, Lydia,
you don't know for sure. You was a girl once yourself," he
said. "Don't hurt to have least one boy to flirt around with."

"You the one said he was too old for her," I said, but
Pemberton swore he didn't know nothing. Pemberton could
be slick when he wanted to. He was the same man took me
all the way to St. Louis without so much as a cricket's twitch
to my daddy about it. I called her downstairs. "Miss October
Brown!"

She come runnin to the top of the steps.

"What is it? What's the matter?" she said.

"Could you come downstairs for a minute, please? Won't
take but a minute."

She come down. The three of us sat in the front room.
Pemberton sat on the divan not saying nothing. He says I lit
into her, but I say I just told her what was what.

"We been keeping teachers for a long time, so I know what
I'm talking about. We been hearing stories, about you and a
young man being at that honky-tonk joint out in the county.
I don't know if you know it or not, but that ain't no place
for a teacher to be seen. People don't want no woman running
around at night and teaching their children in the daytime.

School board don't like it either. We don't want nobody in here going to mess us up with the board. So we don't want to hear no more about it. That's all. I just thought I'd tell you."

The rat can't call the cat to account, so when October Brown got through looking big-eyed at me, she tied up her housecoat and went on back up the steps to her room. Pemberton went on back to the kitchen grumbling about what people is bound to do and what I can't put a stop to.

A couple of Sundays went by. The girls was all nicey-nicey to each other. They come up with the idea that all of them ought to go together to hear Mary Esther and Albertine sing their duet on Reverend Jackson's anniversary program. Jocelyn usually went to Gethsemane and took October Brown with her, but this time they said they'd go hear Mary Esther and those at Strangers Rest. That's me and Pemberton's church, so naturally me and Pemberton went too.

We sat all in one row—Pemberton, me, October Brown, Jocelyn Jones, and Miss Dumas. Albertine and Mary Esther ain't even up there yet when the door opens and a few more folks come in and start finding their seats. Well before Pemberton could get his glasses on good I hunched him so hard he near about dropped them. It was Shorty James Wilson, all right, coming down the aisle with what must have been his wife on his arm, because I don't know no man who would sport a woman fixing to have a baby if she didn't belong to him. His wife was big too, seven months at least. Now I'm sitting right next to October Brown, watching this. I could feel the little jerk she made when she saw them. Blood went right out of her face. You never would've thought it, though, if you hadn't have seen it. She folded her hands in her lap, calm as a stone, and commenced to watch the whole program.

It wasn't my place to say nothing. I suspect she always knew he was married. But now, in front of everybody, she could see for herself what the man cared about. He was coming to church with his family. She wasn't no more to him than a piece of poontang on a Saturday night. I could have warned her about men acting a fool when their wife is big, but you always got to keep the right space between you and the people that live in your house, or else you borrowing trouble.

I gave October Brown credit for cutting Shorty off quick, not wasting a day replacing him. Seems like even the same Sunday she started parting her hair different, putting in some hot curls for a change. Spent near about all her time sewing new skirts and such. Biggest thing, she took to going out Saturday nights. Since Jocelyn went with her, and they wasn't out too late, I figured the girls was having some clean fun. You should have heard them, "How I look in this?" "How you like that?" Regular dolls couldn't have been more prissy. I knew a man was in it somewhere.

Whoever he was, October Brown kept it to herself. She don't want to speak too soon, I thought. Lordy, she swooned and carried on around here.

Tickled me watching her. I figured he was somebody up in Topeka somewhere, because I noticed she started packing up a lunch each time, probably to take on the bus. Keeping it all away from the house was smart. The girls whispered and peeped, but she didn't give them nothing to chew on. It got so most Saturdays she went out early, come back Sundays. Sometimes she'd up and disappear on a Wednesday night too.

Deep in the wintertime I hate going out. It was coming up to my birthday and the girls told me, said I ought to go get my hair done. Every year they took me to the teachers' banquet at the YWCA. I didn't care how good Mattie Donald could do hair, I wasn't going to no beauty parlor in the snow. Well, October Brown said she would do it. Said she used to do her auntie's hair all the time. Looking at hers, I wouldn't have guessed it, but I said okay. Couldn't hurt.

Generally I didn't make a habit of going up to the girls' rooms except once or twice a year to take a look-see or to fix up. I must say, October Brown had done hers pretty. On the table, under the radio, she had laid a little shawl with the fringe, put little lamps and what-nots all around. Crocheted doilies on her armchair. Real pale, blue chenille spread that went with the wallpaper. Right nice.

"Come on in, Miss Lydia," she said. I thought I smelled cloves and I saw orange slices floating in a double boiler of black tea on the burner. I'd done took off my apron and put on the sweater the girls got me for Christmas.

"Don't you look nice," she said, buttering me up. She sat me down in her big armchair, unpinned my braids, and commenced to let all my hair loose.

"I wish *I* had good hair," she said. "I like your silver-gray, just like spun silk around the edges," she said.

My old gray head looking like spun silk.

"You want to take off your earrings?"

I told her no indeedy, Pemberton bought me them gold hoops off a gypsy man over in Missouri one time. Besides my ring, they was the onliest jewelry I ever had.

"I'm going to give you a hot-oil treatment first," she said.

Lord knows I didn't need no grease in my hair.

"It'll loosen up all the old skin on your scalp," she said.

I told her I was old all over, wasn't enough grease in the world to help that.

"Aw, you aren't that old," she said. "I'll bet if Mr. Pemberton wasn't around, the men would still be chasing you. You must have had your pick before you married him," she said.

"Well, I used to could hold my own," I told her.

Truth was I never had a lot of men coming after me, but I got the one I wanted. While she messed around with my hair, I told her about how Pemberton took me from my papa's house in St. Joe and brought me to see Kansas City for the first time. Every life got a little sweet in it, and them were sweet days. Me and Pemberton was young and looking for life. Hadn't even figured out yet that we was livin it. I reckon if Pemberton's daddy's boss man hadn't needed somebody to drive his car to his son in Kansas City, we never woulda got here. Laid back in October Brown's chair, thinking about that time, I'd got so lost I didn't notice how she had done stuck a pillow behind my neck and put a little stool up under my feet. She was working my scalp with her fingers. Near about put me to sleep.

After while she got me up and put me on my knees on a pillow in her straight-back chair at the sink. First off, she did the castile wash. Then she had to use the coconut oil soap. Then vinegar water to cut that. Then it was egg whites for the protein. Lord, when my knees give out she said we was only halfway through. After the egg whites, it was cold water. Then hot water. Then warm water. Then rose water. Finally, she wrapped my head up in a towel she had warming close to the burners. She sat me in the armchair again, parted my hair, and wiped water till I was dead sleep. I'd done laid back and drifted a long time while she fixed around at the icebox.

"Did you ever have any children, Miss Lydia?" she asked.

"Naw, I didn't. Tried two, three times, but none of them made it. Must not have been meant to have them," I said.

"That's too bad," she said, frowning.

"It all happened so long ago, I done forgot."

She changed the subject. "We might as well have a little party while we wait for your hair to dry," she said. She set us out some tiny teacups with flowers all over them and gold at the edges. Laid out a nice little plate of deviled eggs. I don't generally eat deviled eggs in the wintertime, but they was good with the saltines.

"You done already started you a nice life teaching. Think you gonna quit one of these days, raise you some children yourself?"

What did I want to say that for? All of a sudden she stopped chewing and got right up from her chair. Before she could get her face hid she tuned up. Eyes got all big and watery.

"What's the matter, honey? Couldn't be bad as all that. What's the trouble?"

She put up her hand for me to hush, so I did. I waited while she went to the bureau and got a handkerchief to wipe her eyes.

"I think I've done what you asked," she said. "I mean, I've been very discreet, have I not?"

If she was talking about running around and such she was on the mark.

"Yes," I told her. "You been quiet far as this house is concerned."

"Well, now I think I'm going to have to ask you to bear with me."

"For what? This sounds like something I don't want to hear."

"Well, I've gotten myself into a big bind."

"How big?" I asked her. "Don't tell me you done gone and got yourself in trouble."

Well, of course then she didn't say anything. Just wiped her tears.

"Is that it? You're in trouble with the boy? Don't tell me you're pregnant."

That was it, all right. I swear, when I get to heaven, I'm going to ask the Lord why it is that some women can have babies as easy as they can shell peas, and others can't have none, no matter how hard they try.

I told her, I said, "I know my timing ain't too keen, but I told you long time ago me and Pemberton is very careful about stuff like this."

She kept on wiping her eyes and nodding her head yes.

"Well, now the first thing you got to do is you got to be sure the people uptown don't get wind of this. Maybe we can keep you, but only till you figure out what you going to do. Maybe we can hold off a month or so."

"Oh, would you?" she says.

"I'd have to talk it out with Pemberton. Excuse me for saying it, but you ain't in no position to have a baby right now," I told her. I knew too many women done worked it out quietly and nobody was the wiser, but that was between her and the boy.

"Well, what's the boy saying? He want to get married, or what?" I asked her.

She went to crying again. "James says he just needs some more time."

"Wait a minute," I said. "James? What James?"

She commenced to looking like a lamb scared of the shears. "I thought you knew," she said. "I thought . . ."

I'll never understand how she could have held her mouth to let it fall out. The whole thing come clear to me then. It was James Shorty Wilson she'd been seeing all this time. After all that, she'd done played out a plan to get that man away from his wife, and I'd done sat by and let her do it right in my face.

Hairdo or no, I couldn't get out of her room fast enough. But not before I had a little piece of my say to her.

I said, "I should have known. You come in here looking all lost and asking for help, I should have known from the first. Oh, wasn't you smart, come fixing my hair and Oh Miss Lydia ain't we prettying me, sewing them short dresses so you can get that man away from his wife. You must've thought you was cute taking him out of town where nobody could see till you got his nose open good. What did you do? Soak your bloody rag in his coffee? Bake your nappy hair in his cake? Guess that wasn't enough, so you had to go and get yourself pregnant. Well, let me tell you something, you'll not sit your black self up in my house and grin about how you did it, not if I can help it. Shame on you, girl. Shame on the mamma that raised you."

Evil knows where evil sleeps. If she thought she could sneak around and help herself to a man that wasn't hers, she had another thought coming. Me and Pemberton knew the law and if we wanted her out, she had to go. I couldn't cook a pot of water, couldn't eat a crumb until I wrote out the letter me and Pemberton was going to give her.

February 18, 1952

Dear Miss October Brown,

This is to tell you that by February 25, 1952, you have to vacate your kitchenette at 5116 Wynona Ave., Kansas City, Kansas. Our rules say we only rent to upstanding single women with no children. If you are not gone by then, we will take further action.

Yours truly,
Lydia Pemberton,
Thomas Pemberton Proprietors

That evening Pemberton come in ready for his bath. While he run water in the tub, he took off his shirt and throwed it on the bed. That's when he saw the letter.

"What's this?" he said. He knows I don't generally leave mail laying around like that.

"We going to have to put October Brown out," I said. I commenced to tell Pemberton all of what I'd done got out of October Brown that evening. Pemberton was shocked, all right. He shook his head and went on in the bathroom. I suspect he sat in the tub over a hour. I know the news got him because he whistled low like he do when something big is on his mind.

He come out the bathroom and put on his robe, said he wasn't going to eat with the girls that evening. Had him one helping of limas and little bitty piece of corn bread. That was all. He sat in the front room and read the paper while me and the girls ate. Course October Brown didn't come down at all.

That night all that nervous quietness in the house must have woke me up. Must have been two or three in the morning—Pemberton sleeps sound like he's dead except he'll turn over every now and then—I woke up and he was laying on his back with his eyes wide open like he's sure enough dead. I hunched him.

"Lyddy," he says, he don't even blink. "Don't you think we ought to just stay out of the whole thing? Let October Brown keep her room till the school year is out or least till she has a chance to figure out what's what? They's bound to let her go at the school, and she's bound to go back to Ohio to her people. And if by some big miracle, she don't get fired, she still got to go to her people, just later on probably. Seem like to me we ought to keep her till then."

Poor Pemberton. He don't think straight sometimes.

"The word's going to get around, Pemberton, then what? Come next fall guess what house ain't going to be on the list?"

"Lyddy, there's always somebody looking for a place to stay."

"Go on back to sleep," I said. "See how you feel in the morning."

By the time morning come, look like Pemberton got back his cheerful self. Woke me up, kissing me on my neck and fumbling around, talking about how we was young as we felt like being. If I hadn't had to get up and start breakfast, I might have took him up on showing me just how young he thought we was. Me and him had us a good ole breakfast of grits and ham before anybody stirred upstairs. He sopped up his gravy, then he opened up the subject of what to do with October Brown.

"You know, Lydia, the chile is in a fix. If Johnnie Mae

Jackson catches wind of anything, you know Reverend Jackson ain't going to take her in over there. No private family we know will take her, either. I been thinking about this all night," he said. "God moves in mysterious ways, his wonders to perform, am I right? Don't it strike you as peculiar that October Brown come to this door, *our* door, *we* the ones took her in? Now here she is bringing a child into the world under our roof. Don't that seem funny to you?"

It seemed like a shame to me is what it seemed, but Pemberton had done cooked up a whole new life for everybody, including me, and I wanted to hear about it.

"Now I know the other roomers wouldn't like it, yet and still wouldn't it be something having a baby around here squealing. If it was downstairs, wouldn't be no trouble. Me and you both home practically every day. We got the one empty room off the kitchen don't nobody usually want. What if by some streak of luck—not that she deserves it—but say October Brown could save her job, just till the end of the year, which is right around the corner. Next term, maybe they'll hire her over in Missouri. A little child needs a decent place, and that's just what we got here."

I could see wasn't no messing around with Pemberton no longer. He'd done gone clear off with it, like I was just talking to hear myself. Evidently he couldn't understand how bound and determined I was. It was the principle. Without another word I went straight into the bedroom and got the letter, put it square in front of him on the table and give him the ink pen. "Sign it, Pemberton," I said.

He looked up at me like I had a extra head on my shoulders. "You been knowing me almost my whole life," I said. "You ought to know as long as I'm living and breathing, I'm not having no bastard child under my roof. October Brown might do fine, but not in my house."

Pemberton left the letter laying on the table. He moped and scoped around a while. Next day he told me, said, "All right, Lydia. I guess you got a right to grow old in a quiet place if you want to. But we ain't going to put her out yet. She's going to stay here till the summertime, unless she gets married, or goes on back to Ohio or something. We can't kick her out into the street. It ain't right."

"You still got it wrong, Pemberton," I told him. "She ain't staying a minute past Thursday."

"Naw now, Lydia. You done got your way about everything else so just let it alone. The girl is going to stay here till her job is out or they fire her. Ain't no need in us putting no more stumbling blocks up for her."

I never seen Pemberton so stubborn about somebody else's business.

"Pemberton," I said. "I'm going to tell you this one more time. First place, she ain't no girl, not no more. Second place, she ain't no decent woman. And number three, I don't want her here and that's the end of it."

With all the commotion the next couple of days, I knew she was going. By Saturday she'd done brought in orange crates and newspaper. She cooked up there in her room and her and Jocelyn ate up there. Mary Esther was big-eyed and teary every night at the table.

You might know Albertine done figured out some of it. "I don't see why October Brown wants to move closer to the school. There isn't a nicer place up there, unless of course she's not saying what else is going on," she said.

But Pemberton, he was the one acted a pure-D-fool. Friday night I fixed him some greens, baked a whole ham, candied up some sweet potatoes, and cut up a little onion and tomato like he likes. If he touched a crumb my name ain't Lydia. He put on his coat just as big and drove the car over to the dinette. I know because he come back in here with a pig foot sandwich. Sat right up in my face and ate it without saying a word.

I told him, "Mister, you mess around and both of y'all going to be eating pig feet together somewhere, you embarrass me like that in front of the roomers again. You can act a fool if you want to, but it don't change nothing."

He went on in the room. I looked at him sitting on the bed. We was both getting old. We didn't have no business fighting. First thing you know, people would be talking about *us*. I didn't know what got into Pemberton, but I wasn't going to let that girl mess over us.

That Monday, Pemberton went fishing. Like he didn't want to be around. Came back with a whole mess of croakers I cleaned and fried. He ate and never said a word.

Wednesday come, he sat right at the other end of the table and ate his breakfast. Didn't say nothing, but he ate. Got right up and left out. I heard the truck leave and figured he was gone to the plant. When he come in, he had a sack from the hardware place. Took it up and set it outside October Brown's door. Then left out again and was gone the whole rest of the day.

October Brown and Jocelyn come in with more crates and newspaper, flitting and flying around most of the evening. Pemberton went up and down a few times with the hammer or a screwdriver, helping them.

Thursday come and nobody come down for breakfast. Mary

Esther and Albertine both said they didn't have time. Old Miss Dumas didn't want nothing but hot water and lemon. Pemberton swallowed a sausage and biscuit and went right on upstairs. I figured it must be moving day because October Brown and Jocelyn stayed home. With Pemberton helping, they pushed around the furniture, talked, and carried on like they was kin. I got out my embroidery and sat in the front room.

About ten in the morning, Pemberton loaded some stuff in the truck and left out. I hadn't heard where October Brown was moving to. Next thing, Pemberton pulled up in front of the house, and Mr. Carter was riding with him. October Brown come down first, wearing pants, hair tied up in a bandanna, carrying a crate full of linens. Pemberton come in, went on back in the bedroom, and closed the door.

Look like October Brown carried more stuff out than she brought when she came. Her and Jocelyn made ten or twelve trips carting stuff together. Passed by the front room like I was a chair sitting there. Carter stayed outdoors in the truck, fixing the stuff in the back so it wouldn't fall. Finally I guess they was through because they didn't come back in. When the truck didn't leave, I looked out the window. All three of them—October Brown, Jocelyn, and Mr. Carter—was standing there, leaning against the truck, looking at the house. Then, lo and behold, here comes Pemberton out the bedroom with our old suitcase in his hand and a armful of clothes. He come on through the front room, didn't say a word. Went out the door.

First I thought he looked right silly, call himself going somewhere with one suitcase and two or three changes of clothes. Then when he banged around trying to open the door, I thought he was acting like a spoiled child trying to get his way. I decided to teach him. Let him go ahead on.

The picture I can see clear is Pemberton in the back of the truck, and Mr. Carter driving, pulling off with October Brown and Jocelyn up front. Pemberton sitting on a crate with his elbows on his knees like he's sitting on the toilet. Got on his good shirt and Sunday shoes, riding up the street.

Jocelyn come back, but Pemberton didn't. Not yet. Reverend Jackson is letting them stay over there. I imagine Johnnie Mae is having a time with that. Of all people, she's on Pemberton's side about the principle of the thing. They can keep their principle. Pemberton'll be back. He acts a fool sometimes, but he'll be back.

A MOST
SERENE
GIRL

I ALWAYS WONDERED if she saw her father's eyes in that split second before she saw the knife. Did her mother scream, or whimper, or silently consent? Did she see black-red bloom into the fabric of her mother's dress? Was it a summer cotton with lavender flowers and a scalloped collar? The crimson bud opening just above the belt with its flower-covered buckle, the bright red on the handle of the knife, on his shoes—did she see?

Dorla Wooten was the most serene girl in all of Lincoln Junior High. I never saw her talk behind anyone's back. She never got loud in the lunchroom, or ran wildly when we changed classes. In the halls she glided along close to the walls with her head up and eyes straining forward as though something in the distance had caught her attention. And if you said anything to her, she looked down.

Every day in homeroom I made a point of saying, "Hi, Dorla." "Hi, Irene," she would say to the floor. And if I said something more, like, "I like your shoes, did you get them at Robinson's?" she would say, "Thanks," and halfway smile or just say, "Um-hmm." She still wore her hair parted in the middle and braided in thin, pinned-up braids without even bangs, because, obviously, without a mother she couldn't get it curled. She wore only navy blue skirts and either white or pale yellow blouses. As far as I could see, she had no friends. She was so brave, so calm in her suffering, I wanted us to be best friends.

One day the second week of school, I asked her where she lived. "Down the hill," she said, as if down the hill were the name of her street.

I told her, "Maybe we could walk together to the bus stop sometimes." I imagined her at my house listening to my mother's record of Rosetta Tharp singing "Sometimes I Feel Like a Motherless Child." But what could I say to a motherless girl whose father had ruined her life?

It had happened in the summer. The story—with the details about how her father had gone berserk over another man, how he had hidden her mother's body in the back of his truck under trash he hauled to the dump, then broke down and confessed—had come out in our *Voice*, on the Police Blotter page. At the time, my mother had called attention to the way they always put the Police Blotter across from Wedding Announcements, and asked me if I knew any children by the last name of Wooten.

"Crazy fool man," my mother had said. "Bet he wasn't even there half the time, didn't want her and didn't want nobody else to have her."

I knew she was thinking about my father. He was working long hours in Olathe and sometimes stayed there overnight.

My new friend, Geraldine Sims, told me that even before the killing, Dorla Jean was a quiet girl who stayed to herself. Geraldine knew because she and Dorla lived a few blocks apart and went to the same church. She told me that Dorla's mother used to go there too, but that she had never seen Dorla's father, the killer.

After sixth period one day I stole silently in step with Dorla and, like her, kept my eyes straight ahead.

"I hate to catch the bus every evening," I said softly. "I have to wait forever, and nobody lives out my way."

That was not entirely true. Those strange Red Quander children from Redtown with their long dresses and head wraps always rode my bus, then walked the rest of the way. Cece did too, but she hung around with too many boys. Wanda from across the street was always available, but she was in ninth grade, a position from which she was certain to look down and trivialize everything I did.

I didn't think Dorla would quibble in her mind over these facts, but I got no response, not even the blink of an eye from her.

"It would be nice to have somebody to walk with," I said. Again Dorla said nothing.

"You go down Sixth Street?" I asked her.

"Uh-uh," she said, and shook her head.

I thought that she might have to go straight home and I said, "Maybe I could walk down the hill with you."

From the way she shrank back from me, you would have thought I had said something awful to her. Finally she looked at me, but only for an instant. I thought she was sorry for acting so standoffish but, "Uh-uh, that's all right," was all she said.

I told her to let me know if she changed her mind. At that she looked at me again and smiled. I thought it meant, "Irene, you're okay with me."

"I'll walk with you, Irene," Geraldine said, walking behind us. "I like to go down Sixth so I can see what's on at the Carver."

Dorla kept walking, looking ahead.

"Bye," I said to Dorla.

That day Geraldine and I went inside the Carver, a theater reputed to be heaven to rats, rodent and otherwise. We pinched our noses against the smell of urine, drank water from the fountain, listened while hands and voices shot craps somewhere beyond the screen, and when our eyes adjusted to the dark, observed the hollow dilapidated barn with nailed-down seats. Unimpressed, we left, swearing that we'd never be caught dead in there, no matter what was playing. Geraldine and I dated our friendship from that second week of school.

It was also during that second week that girls always brought out their new clothes. Geraldine and I discovered that we both had pink blouses with baby-doll sleeves. We both thought Clyde Thompson was the cutest boy. And music? Geraldine and I liked anything by the Platters. She and I swooned together about the present spectacular season, the most romantic of all, Indian Summer. It summoned us to the outdoors like a narcotic and absorbed us in its steady blaze.

One afternoon Geraldine convinced me that if I walked her halfway home, and she walked me to the Third Street bus stop, I could still get home before five o'clock. So instead of rushing to catch the bus, we went out the back door of the school and leisurely made our way down a hill to where the houses were bigger and farther apart than the ones in my neighborhood. We passed the newly restored St. Stephen's Baptist Church, which I had not yet seen. The Presbyterians had sold it lock, stock, and parsonage to the St. Stephen's congregation. We went into the cluttered fruit market, piled high with black grapes, red and yellow apples, purple cabbages, gourds, pumpkins, barrels of beans, sacks of meal. Two men wearing white shirts and small, black beanies covering the crown of their heads stood behind the counter lined with jars of pickles. They sold us two flat-doughnut mamma cookies.

When we got to what we considered halfway, we turned down Everett Avenue to find my bus stop. Geraldine said, "Wait, I want to show you something."

We detoured down a short street where one-story frame houses squatted low to the ground with little or no porches and with tiny yards separated by vine-smothered fences. Directly in front of a small white house, we stopped. I knew immediately where we were. A death-wreath of dried flowers with a pale orchid ribbon hung from the door.

"That's Dorla Wooten's house," Geraldine said. "Her grandmother came to live with Dorla and her little brothers, and she won't let them take the death-wreath down. Isn't it sad?"

At my stop, Geraldine waited for my bus and waved until we could no longer see each other.

For a while, every day, I went halfway with Geraldine and she waved my bus home. Then, carried on the natural current, I became bold about being late and curious about Geraldine's life away from school. I wanted to see the pink record player she bragged about and the corduroy skirts her mother wouldn't let her wear to school. I insisted on walking her all the way home. She flat-out said no.

"Why? You can't have company?" I asked her.

"It's not that," she said. "You probably wouldn't understand even if I told you."

"Told me what?"

"Never mind. Come on. You can walk me home, but you better not say anything."

"About what?"

"About anything. Just come on."

Beyond our accustomed halfway corner, elm and buckeyes leaned over the street, exploding in reds like random madness. Impressive large houses—two and three stories—sat back on sloping lawns. Hedges and marigolds clumped around porches. Burning leaves seasoned the air.

"Close your eyes and give me your hand," Geraldine said. I closed my eyes and she led me by the hand for what seemed a long block without coming to a corner. Finally she said, "Okay, this is it. Open your eyes."

The house rose three stories, rust brick, with a front-to-side porch. Green awnings overhung windows with identical shades pulled down to identical heights. The broad lawn appeared to be freshly mowed and all the hedges were clipped. Beside the front door a modest white sign with black lettering read TOURIST HOME.

"What's that?"

"That's what this house is," she said.

"What does it mean?" I asked her.

"It means that people rent these rooms so they can have someplace to do it," she said and brushed past me. It shut me right up.

"It's Miss Jones's house. We live in the basement."

She led me into the yard around a narrow concrete path to the enclosed back porch. Inside we took one of two doors and followed a steep stairway to the basement.

"You can't hear anything down here," she said.

The entranceway looked like a half-kitchen. At the far end, a sofa, chairs, tables, lamps, and various other furniture filled the large space. In between, two beds stretched behind folding screens along the stone walls opposite each other. Despite linoleum and rugs, the room felt damp.

Geraldine pulled the fine chain of the light above one of the sleeping areas and turned back the screen.

"Here's my skirt I told you about." She pointed to the open door of her chifforobe.

"And there's the record player." It was a portable, fastened shut. I noted that it wasn't pink, but told her how much I liked the skirt and her house. Neither of us looked at the other. What exactly was there to hear in a place like this? I felt stupid for not having known what the sign meant, and guilty for having made Geraldine explain. Relief overwhelmed the sympathy I wanted to feel for her having to live in a house nobody would want to admit to. Our makeshift, ramshackle furniture and broken plumbing at home dwindled in significance compared to this.

She started to open the record player. I wanted only to leave. She offered to walk with me to the bus stop but I wouldn't let her. "That's all right," I told her, "I've got to hurry."

When I got to the front of the house and looked at the sign, sympathy washed over me.

STOPPING BY GERALDINE's house became my routine. We taught each other a lot of things, not the least of which was how to do the turkey hop. We would be popular, no matter what. We tried whatever we thought would make us into two pretty brown girls: we tamed Geraldine's fly-away hair with red-hot bumper curlers and Hair Rep. For her gangliness that even weight couldn't erase, we agreed that she should always wear full skirts and long sleeves. My tight croquignole curls begged to be fluffed up, and since my calves were thickening a little, I could shorten my skirts. We tested every conceivable shade of lipstick to find one that didn't make our lips look bigger. I probably spent three out of five afternoons during the week in that damp basement.

If you took the other door on the back porch, you could go even deeper into the mystery that was a tourist home. Eventually inside Miss Jones's back door, Geraldine and I slipped past Miss Jones's kitchen and took the stairs to a higher floor and hallway, and still higher to the third floor, apparently unused, with its three locked rooms and storage area. From a window in the storage area I could see our school, dignified-looking in the conflagration of trees. The low street of Dorla Wooten's house left a gash in the view. Electric lines stretched like a web that periodically discharged flashes of electricity as the trolleys moved up and down Fifth Street. Like a flame atop a giant candle, a flickering yellow fire crowned the stack at the refinery near the river. Though I could see it only in part from the high window, my house stood oddly unfamiliar in a row of others. I imagined how homey our front room and kitchen would look to Geraldine's eyes, how pretty my mother would look with her new cut bangs, opening the door and smiling with her beautiful teeth and the beauty mole on her chin.

The appeal of the view from the third-floor window didn't last long. Geraldine grew impatient when she saw me day-dreaming and moved on to the secret activities of the second floor.

"You have to be real quiet," Geraldine said. "The last time I got caught up here, Miss Jones told my mother we had to move."

Except for light from the bathroom, the hallway was dark. We tiptoed on the rug past the doors, pausing at each to listen. I was unsure about what we might hear, but when we heard the slightest noise, we looked at each other with hands clamped over our mouths, nervous, pretending to be amused. Some of the small keyholes were placed just right. That first afternoon, Geraldine and I saw a man buttoning his shirt. Nothing more. But that was enough to whet our determination. A tour of the second floor became an automatic part of any day that I walked Geraldine home and Miss Jones left her kitchen.

One rainy day, we moved quietly from door to door, listening for whatever might bring the rare reward of a man's bare torso through the keyhole, or the equally exciting rush when a woman paraded in her slip. Though Geraldine and I never discussed this, whenever we heard serious noises, like moans or cries, we didn't look, even if the beds were within eyeshot of the keyholes.

This particular afternoon, perhaps because the day had been dreary, or because, as Geraldine said, this was Friday and Friday was payday, we made a promising discovery—five of the rooms held temporary tenants. We decided to keep a continuous vigil, although with so many people coming and going at different times we were taking the risk of being caught.

We began at the safest end of the hallway, deciding that if we worked our way to the far end and a door opened, we could escape up the front stairs to our third-floor haven. When we got to the second door, Geraldine looked first and from the way she immediately drew in her breath, I knew that I had to see too. I signaled for her to move, but she just waved me away. I nearly pushed her over and stooped, my eye wide for the keyhole.

They stood near the wall. In that first instant, I could see only his dark arms enveloping her. With her back to the door, she was a naked brown sheath of curves. They were a twist of fudge and caramel. He lifted her leg, and they nearly lost their balance. They chuckled. Suddenly when he bent forward, I saw a face I had never seen before. And when he swept her off her feet, I saw her face too. The cut bangs and the beautiful profile filled my entire view. She was not a stranger.

My hand froze on the doorknob.

"Don't!" Geraldine whispered, and swatted my hand, jiggling the knob. The man said something very close to the door. Confused, I flew toward the rear stairs. Geraldine flew in the opposite direction. I took the steps down by two's without a thought to noise or Miss Jones.

By the time I met Geraldine I had my plastic rain cape and books in hand, heading up the basement stairs to the bus stop. I insisted that she not walk with me, I needed to get home.

IN THOSE FIRST few days afterward, I couldn't bring myself to look at my mother. I'd get up early, make pressed-ham lunches fast, and get out of the house to catch the earlier bus. Sometimes I'd get to school and have to wait an hour for the doors to open.

"Where you going so early?" she'd ask as she combed Bea's hair.

"I've got to get a book from the library."

"Why you leaving so soon?"

"Got to meet my friend Geraldine."

"Ain't it awful early?" my father would ask.

"I don't want to be late."

And at first I couldn't look at Geraldine, either. I let her think I was upset by the crudeness of what we had seen, fearing that she would sense the real reason I had run away.

"I'm sorry, Irene. I didn't think something like that would make you so mad."

"I'm not mad," I told her. "I just didn't like it."

"If I'd known that, I wouldn't have taken you up there in the first place. Grown people do all kinds of stuff. I guess I'm used to it."

"Do we have to keep talking about it?" I asked her. She was happy to oblige. She didn't press me to come over and I didn't correct her mistaken impression that the shame ought to be hers for living in that house.

Gradually, a curiosity set in that kept me studying my mother. If her hand hesitated in the middle of an ironing stroke, as if something had occurred to her, I wondered what it was. Late afternoons, if I found her stretched across her bed, reading *True Story* magazine, wiping tears, I wanted to know what the story was about. Sometimes she worked a crossword puzzle from the newspaper, then threw the paper and pencil aside with a sigh. What did that mean? She stared at the wall, or out the window at the telephone wires draped across the sky. Sometimes she closed off everything in the outside world and appeared to be looking at nothing. Whenever I interrupted to ask her a question, she would wait the tiniest fraction of a second before she looked in my direction.

She studied me in such a way that I knew she was focusing on the air surrounding me and bringing that look to rest on my face. Then her focus would dissipate like the vapor trails the new jet planes made flying high over our house, and she wouldn't answer. I was afraid she was *that* happy. I was afraid she was *that* sad.

For a short while the routine of school distracted me from worries about my mother. One particular morning our civics classes met to view Civil Defense films. It was a common practice that whenever two classes got together in Study Hall, we all doubled up in our seats. Geraldine and I sat together.

As soon as the lights went out, I felt queasy. I whispered to Geraldine that I thought I was getting sick.

"You want to go to the lavatory?"

"Maybe," I whispered. "I'll wait and see."

On the screen, boys and girls hid under desks as the Civil Defense warning sirens whined. Throngs of people in New York City formed themselves into orderly lines and walked swiftly down into subways-turned-shelters. Farmers in Nebraska ran with their families to bunker-in-the-hill bomb shelters stocked with canned goods.

My stomach churned. I raised my hand for permission to be excused, and my hand became a black silhouette pressed against the cloud mushrooming on the screen. Everyone laughed. My stomach churned. Warm saliva filled my mouth and before I could get a word out, my stomach spewed up all its awfulness. With my hand clamped over my mouth, I tried to make it to the door. Another churn and Geraldine stood dripping my foul-smelling curds from her hands and skirt. Her eyes watered and she too erupted all over the desk and floor.

On our way to the bus stop we laughed at the way everyone

had moved away from us. How the school nurse hadn't wanted to touch us, how we could easily stay out of school for at least another day.

When I got home and described how I had come to be dismissed in the middle of the day my mother had me recount everything I had eaten for days. "Probably ptomaine poisoning," she said. She gave me two doses of slippery elm and sent me to bed.

That evening it rolled in on me the way roiling storms rolled across our corner of the plains—silent, darkening the sky, then rumbling their warning. This was no ordinary headache on its way. The rumble picked up in the space behind my eyes. It got sharper and spread to my temples like a rhythm in a brittle shell, a perfect thunder. My skull surrendered in a million hairline cracks, nerves hurrying pain all over, even to the edges of my teeth. People used to say that sometimes you can be saved by the noise, that you can hear a tornado's roar and take cover. I found no escape from the roaring pain. The room rocked gently, moved sideways. Then the furious finger of God dipped down and swept me away.

I cannot see the flames crackle, but I know the big house is burning. Here the room is tall, wide with smoke, and a voice, your voice, Mamma, is clear in my head. Where are you? I am in the long hallway now, but you cannot see me. I cannot find you. Now the hallway is green. Are you here somewhere on this wide green lawn? Is that your voice I hear? There is a tree, no, a stump. Is that you sitting there? Lavender blossoms around you? Where are your arms? Your body is sliced clean. Circles inside circles—pink, red, liver brown. Your dress, your delicate dress stained red. Your knees crossed, spilling body over them. The pale orchid ribbon that hangs from your waist must be tied in a bow, but my fingers cannot

*move, my arms cannot reach far enough to tie the ribbon, lavender,
blooming red into it from your waist.*

COLD. AT FIRST I felt a shock of cold, then saw the blur of
my mother's face. As words left her mouth, they went in the
direction of an invisible bridge to me, but they traveled on
currents that dipped into the dark below and were lost. I could
focus a little, but everything my fingers came to rest on—the
blanket, her hand—swelled bigger than I could grasp, and I
continued to drift.

"I think she's coming around," I could hear my mother
saying.

I felt the too-cold cloth on my forehead again. Junie and
Bea blurred around the soft island of my mother and father's
bed, where I lay.

"Dr. Reed is on his way. Can you tell me what hurts? You
never been this sick."

I touched my head.

"You scared me. You been talking all out of your head like
you was having a nightmare with your eyes open."

Dr. Reed arrived. "B.C. headache powders. Give her a dose
every six or eight hours until the headache is gone. If she has
one of these fits again, call me. Otherwise bring her in a few
days from now."

For several weeks I stayed home from school. By day, I felt
fine. I wanted to go to school. I read my books, talked to
Wanda and to Geraldine the few times that she caught the
bus to my house. But I hated to see the sun move toward
evening. By dusk each day, pressure formed in my head like
a storm in the atmosphere. Then, on too many nights, I'd be
swept away to the burning house and the green lawn bearing

the solitary stump of my mother's body. Always I would come to myself in some other part of our house, embarrassed not to know how I had gotten there. Sometimes in the middle of the night I would come suddenly awake outside in the yard with my mother or my father shaking me.

"What's my name!" she would ask. "Tell me who I am! Tell me where we are!" Silly things you say to a crazy person. Once I was myself again, I could say perfectly well who she was and where we were, and usually I just wanted to go inside before lights came on in all the neighbors' houses.

With me at home feeling weak but calm, my mother also seemed glad for the daytime. She fed me soup and kept me near her, wrapped in a quilt in the easy chair that she moved from room to room. All the while she watched me, as if she believed that some expression or gesture of mine would yield the key to the mystery of those tormented episodes.

"You know, when you're having one of those fits, you say things that don't make no sense," she said.

I sat propped in the easy chair, out of place in the kitchen where she ironed. Neat stacks of finished sheets and pillow-cases weighed down the kitchen table.

"All I know is that it feels like I'm dreaming, but not like I'm really asleep. And it feels scary. I'm running around scared, then you wake me up," I told her.

I didn't dare think about the rest of the nightmarish images, let alone speak about them.

"Has anything happened that you can't tell me about? Something bad maybe?"

"Nothing that I can think of," I said.

My mother unwound the damp wad of a white shirt, laid it collar-first on the ironing board.

"This shirt don't look like it's clean," she said, and began ironing it. I went on figuring out topic sentences in my English book.

"Sometimes it's like you're talking to yourself," she said. "Sometimes you holler for me. Sometimes you holler for that child Geraldine."

"I don't remember anything like that," I said. It was true.

My mother creased a sleeve. "Geraldine and you, y'all getting to be pretty tight?"

"I like her all right," I said.

"She seems like a decent girl, coming all the way over here on the bus to see you."

"She's all right."

"Who are her people? What's her mamma's name?"

"Miss Butler is all I know."

"She said she had to catch the Fifth Street bus, where do they live?"

"Over Willow Ridge way," I said.

"Where 'bouts?"

"I don't know the house number, but it's on Willow Ridge."

"You been going over that way?"

"I just walk Geraldine home sometimes on the way to my bus."

"Way over there?"

"It's not that far from school," I said.

My mother ironed the other sleeve and turned the shirt lengthwise on the board to press the front.

"They rent or own?"

"I think they rent, a basement kitchenette. It's just Geraldine and her mother. Her father doesn't live with them. They do as good as us, though," I said. "Geraldine's got a chifforobe full of clothes, and her own portable record player."

"Oh, so you been to their house?"

I studied my book and didn't answer. My mother set the iron up on end and looked in my direction, not right at me.

"Where on Willow Ridge you say they live?" she asked.

I didn't know how to answer, so I said, "I get the houses mixed up."

She finished the shirt, put it on a hanger, and hooked the hanger over the back of a chair. She shook out another shirt and ironed it without asking me anything else. Then she unplugged the iron, set it on its heel to cool, and buttoned the shirt onto a hanger.

She said it softly to the space between us, like she was sharing bad news: "They must room in one of those big brick houses, huh?"

"I don't think it's brick," I said.

She went into her bedroom off the kitchen. I sat looking at my English book until my father came home from work.

Dr. Reed attributed the whole situation to menstrual problems. "Some girls get it bad," he said. "You know, headaches, tension, crying spells. Didn't you say she just started having periods a few months ago? She's still at the starting end. She'll get over it."

And I did. After a long while, the force of the storms died down, they grew further apart, then stopped altogether. No longer dreading the sunset, I was relieved to be back to my normal self. My mother and father seemed relieved too.

At school everything had changed. All the girls wore a new kind of lipstick—frosted, they called it—that didn't look so hot, but I thought I could get used to it. And a new hairstyle had swept through Lincoln. That was all right, because I had simply to comb my curls back and push and I would have the full, deep waves everyone was wearing.

Clyde Thompson wasn't nearly as cute as I remembered. He started making noises like he wanted to walk me to the bus stop, and once in a while, in the cold wind of short November evenings, I let him.

Geraldine and I saw each other only at school, and then, only in class. She said it was my fault that we were drifting apart, that since Clyde got interested in me I didn't care about her. Although I didn't tell her, she seemed uninteresting, plain, more like Dorla Wooten. I didn't feel close to her anymore. And I guess I just didn't want to be around anybody who lived in a tourist home.

One day in the lunch line Geraldine asked me to go to Dorla Wooten's house. "Dorla's grandmother is letting her have a birthday party with boys Friday night. You want to go?"

"I don't think so," I said.

Geraldine turned around to Dorla, who was a few places behind us in line and made cryptic signs. Then a note made its way up the line from Dorla through Geraldine to me. "I hope you can come to my party Friday night," it said.

"Why don't you come and bring Clyde," Geraldine said.

"I don't think so," I told her.

"Why not? Dorla's really nice. She likes you."

"Dorla is a frone girl. She's always moping around," I said. "And besides, she acts like she's the only person on earth anything ever happened to."

Who wanted to hang around with a girl who didn't even wear lipstick or get her hair curled? Who wanted to go to a party in a house that once had a death-wreath hanging on the door?

THE GREAT
WAR

It is dusk. You could say that every time Pearlean has come out to sit on her front porch, every time she has sat in the flamingo-pink glider that, with every rocking glide, squawks from its warp of metal on metal, every time she has brought her comb and brush and sat in the glider combing her just-washed hair, every evening that she has painted her toenails pink on the porch while she watched the children play hopscotch, every single evening after ironing tablecloths and pinafores all day, after laying white shirts out on the table to sprinkle and roll like white jelly rolls to be ironed and on hangers all turned the same way by six o'clock when cars drive up and collect the blouses and skirts, the white shirts with not too much starch and, Lord no, no blueing, no bleach—all those evenings after all those days, you could say that she has been waiting.

In the first long wish with the whole world, she waited for him to come home from the jungle in New Guinea where some men died and others went crazy over the native women. But she waited for him and went one better. Still a girl herself, she waited for their baby girl, waited for the baby that came wailing into the world proclaiming that here and now their lives would begin together.

But she had to wait for him to get a steady job, maybe in Sedalia, or else they couldn't eat. While she waited she made baby clothes, curtains for their one window, vanity skirts, made dough-cakes to save money, and lemon meringue pies to sell, whittled stick-men from birch branch, made do and waited. And when they were paying double for bricklayers in Olathe, and paying next to nothing for hauling coal here, she said, sure, it was all right, she would wait.

Surely it was only a matter of months until they got on with living, until the company got the building built, or the sidewalk laid, or the retaining wall finished. He was a good husband, paid three months' rent in advance, bought them a new bed. Sweet man, hot love, couldn't keep his hands off when he was home. When he was home. Sure, she could wait. She had the baby to play with. But what does a woman do with the feelings that bubble up when she's rubbing herself in the tub, or listening to Billy Eckstine on the radio? "I love you," she said. "Wait until I get on my feet," he said. "Won't be long."

Then there was the next baby. A long wait for a fertile body to make little legs and fingers, good eyes, and the best-shaped head. A long wait.

And every one of those hundreds of days filled itself up with small waits—for the iron to heat up, the skillet to sizzle, the child to get home from school, Sunday to come, payday, a word, a glance, the truth.

She's wondering this evening, now that the iron is standing cold on the board in the kitchen, and she's sitting in the glider that rocks like a squawking flamingo on the porch. She looks at her long legs. What good is love when you sit alone and wait?

Sure she waited. Because the woman she heard he was going with was pretty. Smarter than the two of them put together, really. She waited because he belonged to her, because the woman probably didn't want him anyway, because no man can keep a woman and a wife happy at the same time, because whatever goes over the Devil's back has got to come under his belly, because he was a decent man who would always do right by his kids, because what else could she do but wait?

And he came back. But since the best work was either on the railroad runs from Chicago, where he would have to live, or at the packing house across the river, where he would have to work the late shift, there was nothing to do except sit on the porch. And since every friend she ever had was busy and nothing good was on the radio, she went to church. Sunday. Morning, afternoon, evening Baptist Training Union. Singing in the women's chorus. Singing "Christ Is All" at prayer meeting Wednesday night, Friday night Circle. What does a woman say when a nice man who has a nice job at the Post Office says that a young woman like her ought not to wait alone?

What was a husband, really? What good was a hip-husband-jitterbug with a wide-brim hat and stitched-sole Florsheim shoes? What kind of man-child-husband was this smooth talker who knew every word the King Cole Trio ever sang but didn't know his wife had a birthmark on her behind? What kind of husband-hands couldn't go slow in the fresh sheets, what kind of husband-mouth laughed at her when she put her foot down about out-of-town jobs?

The eventide falls fast and she's waiting on the porch thinking about all that time. And isn't this the Post Office coming now, showing off his new used Chevrolet? Smiling and waving, isn't this him? And around the block to smile and wink one more time. She ought to hard-press her hair with the new bangs they are wearing. What if she winks back and recrosses her legs? What if she goes into the house to wait by the party-line phone for this Post Office man to call?

He has promised her a Mixmaster. He swears that nobody will know. And even if someone discovers their secret, who would blame them? His wife is old. Forty already. Frigid, he says. He needs a real woman. He can smell the wait getting short in her, he has seen her on the porch with her bowl of ice cream.

It is dusk. Everything is suspended. A day that started brilliantly and burned along a steady course, now treks so deeply into darkness that it has lost its way. Pearlean combs her hair. Her husband is working late. Who does she love? What is love, anyway, but a silly, groundless thing she made up in her head. Once it was handsome, tender, kind, rich, smart. Once it could sing sweet, talk good, pray out loud, and surely dance. What is it made of? What is there to love? What is there in anyone to love?

SECRET

LOVE

WHEN SHE WAS sixteen-going-on-twenty, and I was fourteen-back-pedaling-to-twelve, for no apparent reason Wanda suddenly stopped letting me read her diary. We were upstairs in her bedroom—a triangular attic room with a tiny window, bare beams, and a speckled linoleum floor. She sat subdued on her studio couch because she was just getting past a bad time with her brother, Puddin. We were listening to her FM and talking about a boy she liked when I asked her if she had written anything about him in her diary. "I'm not doing that anymore," she said.

If I had to name a single thing that I took for granted those days, it would have been reading the stories of Wanda's life. Every conceivable thing about her could be found in that five-year journal so thick with extra pages that the clasp would not hold and the whole thing had to be bound with rubber bands. For the most part, my friendship with her had been a condition of living cata-corner from their house, a convenience. Not that it mattered to her. She wouldn't have noticed that I resented the way she rubbed her experiences like salt into what I can only describe as my bland, open naïveté.

Aside from appreciating their shock value, I had come to tolerate those stories as possible glimpses into my own future.

I couldn't believe that she would no longer keep track—cell by cell—of "being a woman," or that she would fail to document her epiphanies about love. This was the same Wanda whose whole outlook on life was autobiographical.

Undoubtedly such a fixation on herself came from her mother. Mrs. Coles seldom missed an opportunity to praise her daughter or, for that matter, her less fortunate son. She often referred to them as strong-willed.

"Puddin's strong will is what keeps him going," she would say. Or "Wanda might be tiny, but she's got a strong will. And thank God she's got her daddy's looks."

Those times when Wanda convinced me to come over just to keep her company, I never got away without fielding at least one of her mother's requests.

"Look at her, Irene. You tell her. She's got beautiful hair, doesn't she?" And she would brush Wanda's hair away from her face or sweep it up in the back.

And Puddin. Mrs. Coles was so ambitious for his smallest success that she outright ignored his misbegotten state. Say a neighborhood child came riding up on a tricycle. If Mrs. Coles and Puddin were outside sweeping the sidewalk as they often did—her with a regular broom and him, big as any man and making wild motions with a stick—she would seize the chance for him. Despite the fact that Puddin usually abandoned his own toys, she would say, "Puddin can ride that, can't you, sweetheart? Let him try."

Everywhere she went, she brought him along, and he was as content with eating out of his jar of mayonnaise as a baby would be with a nipple. People stared. When he made his cicada sounds too loudly, those who didn't know him were leery. At the grocery store it was not uncommon for Mrs. Coles to smile at such people, then coerce them into letting Puddin carry their groceries to their car nearby. Most of her intercessions worked out peacefully enough. But occasionally he would ruin a toy or throw a whole bag of groceries to the ground at his pleasure. Still, people understood and made allowances. "She'll never cut the cord," my mother said.

Their father had been Creole from Louisiana, and though, as my mother reminded me, he had a lot of "us" in him, it all came together in the smooth, light complexion and straight hair he passed on to his daughter. Not that my mother had anything good to say about looks. Cleanliness, intelligence, yes, but she ignored prettiness. According to her, good sense was the answer to everything. And to her way of thinking, Wanda was born to be fast.

Days before her final declaration in the attic, Wanda had flipped to a page and handed me her fat, tan journal. "Look at last Friday," she said. She might have suspected that I kept a diary, and who knows, perhaps if she had asked, I would have shared mine. Probably not, though. No matter how moving my entries seemed when I wrote them, next to hers they sounded like so much whining. As usual the "requests only" hour on KPRS played on the radio, and she watched my expression as I read aloud her oversize scrawl:

"And then Jesse Belvin's record, 'Goodnight, My Love' (now my favorite song), came on. They played it twice. The first time Owen was dancing with Sylvia. I stood against the wall and stared him down. The second time they played it, he almost knocked Richard over trying to get to me first. I had on my green skirt with the kick-pleats and my short heels, so I was just the right height. When we slow-danced, he kissed me all the way down . . ."

"Kissed you all the way down—what does that mean?" I asked her.

"You don't know *that*? Reenie, girl, you can be so frone sometimes. Stand up."

I stood up. The wooden ceiling slanted long and low, so that she had to pull me to the center of the room in order for us to stand straight. I was a shade taller and I slipped off my loafers. The cold linoleum floor felt grainy.

"Put your arms around me," she said.

I hugged her around the waist.

"Not like that. You're supposed to be slow-dancing."

I felt silly, but I laid one hand lightly on her shoulder and held the other out—dance position.

"He did me like this," she said.

She flung my arm more tightly around her neck, caught my waist and drew me in, then caught my other hand in hers against her shoulder. We were pressed together, my cheek against her temple. Highlights at the edges of her brown hair brought out the tan of her face. Her skin seemed to be pulled satin-smooth over the square plates of her cheeks, her brown eyes flashed topaz. Her nearly translucent teeth suggested that they were somehow fragile. She smelled like the glycerin and rose water she used as lotion. She had gathered her hair to one side with yellow twine and it tangled in the borealis earrings that dangled from her ears. I felt the small cushions of her breasts between us.

"See," she said. "You can't hardly move, can you?"

I shook my head.

"Boys want you to feel everything they got," she said, and she released me.

For a moment I had the impulse to touch her skin, or her hair. Desire, however, is sometimes the affectionate face of envy, and in the next moment I tried to imagine what might mar those flawless features that nobody could resist.

I never dreamed that a day or two later the ever-so-calm Wanda would be frantic about Puddin. I knew nothing about it until my mother, having seen a police car out front, got it from Cece's mother that they were looking for Puddin. He had wandered away and into trouble out in Washington Heights. According to Wanda, the police accused him of breaking into a house out there and threatening a woman before he wandered away again. Mr. Pemberton from the church had found him first and brought him home.

"Wilma Coles is fit to be tied," my mother said of Wanda's mother. "Must be they're planning to put Puddin away this time. I knew when his daddy died she couldn't handle him by herself. This makes the eleventh dozen time he's done something she can't fix."

Since most of the time I saw Wanda as the model of composure, in full control, I had no experience with the role of comforter. I knocked hesitantly on her door. When she opened it, she said, "Oh," like right then she was expecting the police or maybe she was just surprised that I had come unbidden. She looked smaller than the Wanda I had hugged a few days before.

"Can you come out, or should I come inside?" I asked her.

"You can't come in," she said, too quickly. Then she softened it with "Maybe I can come out for a minute," meaning that she didn't want me there. She came out to the porch and pulled the door behind her.

"I guess you heard about Puddin," she said. Her voice quivered.

I nodded. "Yeah."

Then she told me about the police.

"What's going to happen?"

"I don't know, but Mamma said we'd better not let anybody in the house right now, you know, with Puddin sleeping and everything."

I said I'd see her later and started back across the street. I remember the evening as chilly, with a sun of molten-red lava about to erupt through cracks in the blue-gray clouds. Wanda didn't go in right away. I turned and waved, and the way she lingered there on her porch struck me as strange. All evening I watched to see if the police came back, and when they didn't return by dark, I began to think that they had let it go, that Puddin was safe. Later, when I thought about that evening, I would remember Wanda standing small, guarding her doorway, red in the spilled light of a setting sun.

It had been my intention to check with Wanda the next day about her brother, but when I came home from school, life in my own house had unfolded like a mean chit of time plotting to be remembered.

Aside from my preoccupation with Wanda and Puddin, the day had begun routinely. My father was a temporary worker at the packing house on the noon-to-nine shift. From sunup he piddled in the kitchen or out front with his truck until we left for school. I had grown content that he and my mother had learned how to talk to each other. What had once been raw chunks of conversation flung in the face had at last mellowed to decently thin slices that could be easily swallowed.

And so I was unprepared. My first reaction to the clutter of clothes and shoes in our front room was that my father had been laid off and was packing to find work in Olathe or Sedalia again. Then my mother appeared carrying one of their bureau drawers full of his underclothes.

"Change your clothes and come help me," she said. "Take this upstairs with you." Upstairs everything had been shifted and mixed. Greater upheavals were to come when, back downstairs, she sat me down and showed me a photograph.

I have said that my mother never valued looks. The only photograph she had of herself as a young girl was this one in which she was a pretty fifteen. In the sepia print, she wore a white pinafore dress and white sandals, her hair up in a pompadour. She sat with her legs crossed on the hood of a Ford, a prop "just for the show," she said, but it looked real and she posed like she owned it. That afternoon when she showed it to me for the first time, she said, "I used to be all that."

Then she broke the whole thing open. "Reenie," she said, "I'm not telling you nothing that you don't already know when I say that things aren't so hot between your daddy and me."

My expression must have contradicted her because she said, "Now Ree, I know you been knowing certain things for a long time."

I pretended to study my hands. By "certain things," did she mean the business that had happened at the tourist home? I had learned to bury those and any other dire thoughts deep in my diary, to be examined at some kinder time.

My throat ached. I needed to swallow, or to cough. We were stuck sitting beside each other on her bed.

Then in a huff she said, "We'd better get the rest of this

stuff upstairs." I expected her to finish with "before your daddy gets home," but she didn't.

Junie and Bea came in from school, big-eyed and quiet when they saw the shuffle. Like obedient little windup toys they got peanut butter and stayed out of the way. My mother and I dragged the bureau upstairs and put in the drawers. We each took armloads of clothes, which we hung in the closet and folded in sloppy heaps on the bed. At one point in our questionable enterprise she said softly, "Ree, he's the nicest man I ever met." I ignored this and asked, "Shouldn't we put away the ties and stuff?"

She kept folding things and said, "I know you heard what I said."

I blurted, "What's Daddy going to say?"

She looked off into space, stroking the smooth fabric of one of my father's ties. "He doesn't know," she said, and folded the tie.

"I mean about all this stuff up here, you know, moving it without asking him?"

She frowned as if I had rebuked her.

"Ain't nothing he can say. He should have thought about that when he marched his sorry behind out of here so big. Nobody asked him to come back, either."

I thought about the time years before when he had left us to be with Miss Brown. He had come back, though, and stayed. By my calculations it shouldn't still count against him. Besides, hadn't my mother evened the score?

"Anyway," she said, "he shouldn't be surprised. Women have needs."

I hated that. I hated to hear her say women have needs. I hated that dark sea of mysterious passions women were supposed to have, that apparently made them behave in uncontrollable ways, like in all those magazines. Some women. I was never going to dip into it.

Back downstairs she stacked two sheets, a pillowcase, and a chenille bedspread on my arms.

"Take these up there and make up the bed."

While I tucked sheets and searched for some firm principle to stand on, I heard Wanda's knock. She always hit the door with the flat of her hand. Right then I decided that none of this room-switching was anybody else's business. Especially no one who was obsessive about personal things. Especially not Wanda.

I needn't have worried, she wouldn't have noticed anything. I could see that she had been crying, which meant that Puddin was gone. But in my own confused state that day I had little to give her.

I remember saying "Hi," and her rushing in and sitting on the sofa. It turned out that midmorning, while I was at school, and while my mother had been busy figuring ways to split up our house, they had taken Puddin away. My mother had seen the whole thing. A paddy wagon had come. Two plainclothes policemen had gone into the Coles house. They had come out with Puddin in handcuffs. Mamma said he was making the sound he made whenever he was excited, his cicada sound, and that Mrs. Coles had fallen out wailing on the porch. Mamma had gone over to help Wanda get her back into the house.

When Wanda rushed into our front room, though, she gave no details, saying only that Puddin was gone. "Tomorrow we have to go fill out papers, but he isn't coming home. They're taking him down to Osawatomie."

That name should have summoned up dungeons and turrets in my mind; the town of Osawatomie surrounded the state asylum for the insane. According to everything we heard, it was worse than prison, which was the most horrible place anyone could ever go. But Wanda might as well have said they were taking Puddin for a ride on the merry-go-round for all the impact it had on me. We stood in the front room handling the minutes, touching things probably, and no doubt fueling our separate worries. I don't remember. At any rate, she didn't stay long.

That night, when Armour's nine o'clock whistle blew, it filled the city with the sound of God blowing across the lip of a heavenly bottle. Time for my father to get off work. Nothing eventful occurred those nights when he arrived home. Usually when he hit the door, he called out our names in run-on syllables, "Hey-Bob-a-Ree-Bop-June-Bug-Missie-Bea!" Usually Junie and Bea greeted him with "Guess what we had for dinner," or "So-and-so did thus-and-such at school." Usually he headed right upstairs to wash up, unless it was payday and he passed around candy. Usually my mother warmed his late supper and set it on our yellow Formica table before she retreated to her bedroom and her magazine. He would have his supper with the radio sitting right on the table and us kids gathered to watch him eat. Once he had finished and we were all in bed, I was able to ignore the sounds of the house settling and give myself to sleep.

That unusual night, whether or not he was prepared, one trip upstairs and he discovered the new state of affairs. Junie and Bea had read the signs and hidden themselves away early in their beds. My mother stayed in her room with the door closed. Up to my elbows in dishwater, I stood very still in the kitchen, alert to his footsteps overhead. He came down the stairs slowly, as if he were just waking up. Silence wouldn't do. I snatched the radio from the top of the refrigerator, set it on the table, and plugged it in.

When he got to the kitchen I clanged dishes and banged pans, not daring to look at him. The radio buzzed. I zinged forks and knives into the drawer, splashed water over the stove, rubbed the refrigerator hard. He turned the dial right through the ball game and the fights, all the way to KPRS, then wound it back again.

"Daddy, you want your plate warmed up?" I asked him. He didn't answer.

With serious purpose, I warmed his liver and rice on the stove, made his plate, and ladled the gravy over it just so. I set it before him on the table and put the box of salt beside his glass of iced tea. His stewed tomatoes needed a separate little bowl, his two slices of bread looked better on a separate saucer. He turned to the news. I sat at the table and watched him begin to mix gravy into his rice.

He looked across at me, then blinked recognition, as if suddenly I had burst forth on the air in front of him. Then he zeroed in. So much of what got said was in his eyes and the clench of his teeth.

"Go to bed," were his actual words. But from his whole being I was certain he knew it was I who had taken his clothes to the upstairs closet. That without raising a single objection, I had allowed my mother to be with a strange man in the tourist home. And that I was the one who had made the bed upstairs where he must lie. It was as if he had given me some precious thing of his for all my fourteen years and now he was taking it back.

AGAIN I COULDN'T see telling Wanda. With her mother falling apart, she probably had her hands full and wouldn't have come looking for me anyway. But I suspect that in the back of my mind I wanted Wanda to know that I too had something to lament. After a few days, I went over to see her. I didn't want to be saddled with her reading me that sad chapter of *her* life and me swallowing my own.

Up in her room, she sat on her studio couch and held on to her elbows. I sat on the cold floor and rested my back against the couch.

"What you been doing?" I asked her. I stretched out my legs.

"Nothing. Just sitting up here listening to the radio. Owen sent me a request yesterday."

"That's nice. Everybody's been asking about you at the bus stop. I miss seeing you."

"Yeah, me too. I'm coming back to school Monday."

"What will your mother do without Puddin to take care of?"

"I don't know, and I don't care," she said.

The tone wasn't what I had expected, but I could see how she might feel both anguish and relief at no longer being responsible for him.

"You talk to Owen since the request?"

"No, I can't be bothered with him, either," she said.

"I'll believe that when I see it in writing," I said.

"Oh, I'm not doing that anymore."

"What, no more Owen?"

"I mean I'm through with writing stuff down," she said.

"You mean give up your diary after all this time?"

"Yeah."

"Where is it?" I asked her. I looked around. She always kept her diary under her pillow.

"What did you do with it?" I asked.

"It's put away. Maybe in ten years I'll get it out again."

"I don't believe you," I said. I turned and swept my hand under her pillow forcing the diary into plain sight. We both grabbed for it, but I was quicker.

"Give it here!" she said.

I relinquished the book. "Bad, Bad Whiskey" came on the radio. I remember because it was an awkward moment and I played with an empty glass that sat beside the bed. When the song ended I left.

Over the rest of the week the women in the neighborhood took turns making cakes and casseroles for Wanda and Mrs. Coles, just as if Puddin had died. That Friday my mother invited them over to eat with us. Seldom did we ever have company for dinner, and if I had believed that either of us had normal families it would have been festive. Mamma had fed Junie and Bea earlier and sent them upstairs. She made spaghetti, homemade rolls, and a fruit cocktail salad. I set our four matching plates on the table.

"Come on in, Wilma," my mother said. They had gotten all dressed up—Mrs. Coles in a navy blue dress and black suede high-heel pumps, Wanda in a pink sweater set.

"Goodness," my mother said, "dinner isn't going to be that fancy. I just thought you might like a break from your own cooking. James don't get in till late."

"It was real sweet of you, Pearl," Mrs. Coles said. I heard

the sadness in her voice and understood that this invitation to dinner was our acknowledgment of their loss. Clearly no one should mention Puddin.

Our careful conversation started with the possibility of snow. I had never before taken part in a conversation with a group that included my mother.

"Looks like we'll have snow early," Mrs. Coles said.

"I love the snow," I said, looking around to see if this was the acceptable way to do it.

"We get snow, and your daddy can't work," my mother said, but with a tone that implied concern for more things than just money.

My mind went wild with the possibility that Wanda and her mother might understand the implication in my mother's words: the new sleeping arrangement and the gaggle of secrets surrounding that arrangement. That my mother referred, even obliquely, to that sorry mess seemed careless.

"I remember when Mr. Coles was alive, he hated the snow," Mrs. Coles said. "It made his missing leg ache."

That was enough. Not only had I opened the door to expose our family's failures, but also I had stepped on Wanda's father's grave.

We passed the bowls around the table. Then while trying to explain the salad to Mrs. Coles, my mother made her own faux pas.

"Just add pecans and a couple of apples to a can of fruit cocktail, and stir in some mayonnaise." That last word hung over the table. I was sure that we all thought of Puddin being deprived at the asylum while we heaped our plates.

Finally Wanda said, "I think I'm going to try out for Girls' Ensemble."

The remark was innocent enough, nobody would mind talking about Wanda's talents. But surprisingly, Mrs. Coles put down her fork. From the deliberate way she swallowed her food, I could tell she had something disagreeable to say.

"No, Wanda Jean, you are *not*." She bit each word. "You are in the eleventh grade. It's time you started learning something useful. You have yet to enroll in typing or shorthand."

"And I don't intend to, either," Wanda shot back.

"Hush, Wanda Jean. I *said* you will take typing and that's what I mean."

Wanda straightened her back and narrowed her eyes. "I'd like to see you try to make me," she said.

I held my breath, and I'm sure my mother did too. Visibly, Mrs. Coles's face puffed and she nearly wheezed, but she didn't say anything. Not a word. And Wanda didn't stop there. She sat still a few seconds, glaring at her mother, thinking of something else that would jab her.

"I'm never going to listen to you anymore," she seethed. "Ever."

This would have gotten anyone else I knew at least a slap from across the table. But Mrs. Coles just sat there quietly with her chin in her plate.

"Now Wanda, we can't have all this at the dinner table," my mother said.

"I'm trying out for the Ensemble," Wanda said.

My mother changed the subject. "You know, Wilma, I've been thinking about shorthand classes for Irene next year. They tell me they have waiting lists a mile long. You all care for some iced tea?"

"Yes," Mrs. Coles said and went back to her spaghetti.

As my mother poured iced tea into the glasses, her eyes

danced with self-satisfaction over her correct opinion of Wanda, so clearly proven before us. The exchange between Wanda and her mother was satisfying for me too. I was taken by Wanda's attitude. I could imagine her looking across the table at my mother and saying, "Mrs. Wilson, you need to get yourself together."

Later I told Wanda how impressed I was. "Stunning" was the word I used. For the most part I was sincere. I suppose I thought, too, that she would learn to trust my sympathy for her and over time she would share her diary with me again. But she never did.

She included me, though, in the production she made of going to visit Puddin. Every other Sunday she and her mother left before sunrise to get the 7:00 A.M. Overland bus. Saturday nights she made sure Puddin's box was packed with toys and clothes he might like. And she cooked enough food for ten people! Puddin's chicken had to be fried until it was almost burned and dry—the way he liked it. There had to be mostly red jelly beans in his little jar. She spent days on Minnesota Avenue looking for the kind of harmless toys they would let him keep. Corduroy and flannel were the only fabrics she would consider for him. Some of those Saturday nights I sat up with her.

On one such night Mrs. Coles went to bed early. In the kitchen, Wanda fried Puddin's chicken to a crisp. Two flights up, alone in the attic, I folded corduroys and labeled crayons and coloring books with Puddin's real name—Thaddeus Coles, Jr.—in black ink.

I was passing time. Alone in Wanda's room. The whole thing was a fluke. I looked around her room. Because it was secret, just because it was secret, I felt beneath her pillow. The diary was still there.

I removed the rubber bands all together, and the thing fell open flinging folded squares of extra pages across the bed. In a panic I thought I would never be able to insert them all back into their proper places. I had to try. I unfolded the first one to see the date. "May 6 (continued)," it said. I refolded it, found May and stuck it back in. The next square was thicker, a full-size sheet of narrow-lined paper with writing on both sides. "Nov. 8 (continued)," it said. At the top of the page, Wanda had scrawled the sentence "I hope I did the right thing." And she had repeated it several times like a child's punishment at the blackboard.

I refolded the paper and inserted it into the first week of November. Then more pages, more dates. I hurried. More pages. More dates. *I hope I did the right thing.* I went back to November and quickly scanned her entry for the day before Puddin was taken away.

Mr. Pemberton brought him back, but the police . . . Mamma is really . . . can't believe she . . . serious . . . no matter . . .

Again I unfolded the sheet of paper Wanda had inserted. It said:

Nov. 8 (continued):
    I hope I did the right thing.
    I hope I did the right thing.
    I hope I did the right thing.
    I know she will say it was out of love, but it's wrong. I can't ever prove it even if I wanted to (and I don't), but I know the jar had poison in it. Or else why was she stirring a brand

new jar? And hiding it from me? She wouldn't of put it right beside his bed. She always told him that she would never let anybody take him. This is what she meant. I knew it right away, too, soon as she said go kiss him goodbye while he was sleeping. Telling me not to wake him up, even in the morning. I think she thinks she owns us. I don't know how she's going to act when she finds out that I threw it away, but I don't care. Maybe it's her who can't live without us. Or she just don't want to see him treated so mean. I don't want him treated mean either. I really don't. In case I die and somebody finds this, this part is for you Puddin. Mamma probably loves you much as I do. I don't know. All I know is, if you could of told me you would rather be dead than to go there, I would of let you eat the mayonnaise. But since you can't ever say what you want, I had to do what I wanted. I know they are not going to treat you right down there, but someday I hope you will get out and be happy your still alive. . . .

I never heard Wanda on the stairs. There she was, tall, stark. For the endless seconds that I could look at her, she looked at me. I remembered the paper in my hand and began to fold it. She stood frozen with her hands clutching her elbows while I gathered the rest of the folded pages and twisted the rubber bands around the whole bundle. I held it out to her. Like a chicken with its head chopped off, she flew right at me, and struck in a hard hot fire across my face.

When I recovered she was sitting against the wall near the window, weeping. I sat near her on the floor and wept too.

As THE HOLIDAYS approached, the weather became more severe. I spent most of my spare time with Wanda. I told her about our split house, and when I saw that she really listened,

I wanted her to know how it got that way. And so, for the first time, I let her read my diary.

She filled me in about Puddin. By turns it was hard, then sad, then hard again to believe the gruesome thing about her mother, but Wanda had no doubts. She told me about Osawatomie and the few people there who were like Puddin, and those who weren't. The scary ones she saw, the dangerous ones she heard about. Every other day she thought she wanted to run away with Owen. She made the Girls' Ensemble, which gave her even more reason to be conceited. But she wasn't. Not really.

THE

CREATION

I F I HAD not seen my life sinking in the unhip backwater of high school, I would not have prayed night after night for something big to happen to me, the way it seemed to be happening to everyone else. By everyone else I meant Carol Walker who had to be "stabilized" at the hospital after eating crackers and water for two weeks because her boyfriend quit her. And Wanda. She had become one of the exalted. A senior, and crowned by the entire school when the police caught her drinking liquor at Shady Maurice's, where she placed second in the Friday-night talent show. Not a month went by that I didn't observe Jewel Hicks's wan return to school after being stupefied with morphine her doctor gave her for the cramps. If such events shook up their existences to make those girls aware of living, not a single event disrupted mine. I spent my time walking around looking for something I could not describe, until I found it in the Red Quanders.

I was only six or seven when Dottie, my play aunt from church, first took Wanda and me to the colored lights strung around the pony rides, tubs of cotton candy, and stalls of hit-the-target games we called the carnival. Instead of taking us the long way down Tenth and across Walrond, she walked us along the railroad tracks to the trestle high over the open sewer of Skagg Creek.

"Don't look down at the water or you'll fall in," she yelled, then ran off and left us.

The trestle, higher than Union Hall in Rattlebone, might as well have been a tightrope. Dizzy above the leaden, gray stream, I had nothing to hold on to. I knelt down. Wanda kept walking ahead of me. Then when neither of them would come back, I crawled on hands and knees, afraid to keep my eyes shut, afraid to open them. That's how I got across. That's how I remember the first time I saw Red Quanders.

I passed their strange district as I lagged behind alone. The dozen or so shotgun shacks and outhouses pushed up close to the railroad tracks reminded me of how scared I had been of spiders and daddy longlegs in the outhouse we used before we were hooked up to the city. Long before the day Obadele Quander first knocked on our door selling fresh-dressed chickens, I was passing near his house looking at chicken coops, goat stalls, and gardens, wondering who were all these people living between the tracks and the woods. At the time, nothing was as puzzling as the way all of them had their heads covered in fire-red satin, the men in a do-rag style, and the women in a kind of wrapped gèle.

Finally, my play aunt came back for me.

"Who are they?" I asked her.

"Red Quanders," she said. "This is Redtown and those obeah women will get you if they catch you looking at them, so stop staring and come on."

None of the dark men with braided beards, and none of

the dark women cooking over wash-tub fires seemed to notice us.

YEARS WENT BY. Redtown was there, a part of our part of the city. I was familiar with Folami and Akin, the Red Quanders everybody knew because they went to our high school. They were twins, not identical, but you could tell they were related. Aside from them, I seldom saw any of the others, they seldom came over our way. So what led Obadele Quander to my house that September? And on a Saturday morning, too, when I looked like Hooty Coot in my mother's faded sack dress and my hair not even combed. Of all the doors he could have knocked on, why did ours stand out to him? And when I opened it and he saw my face, did he think of cinnamon, or tobacco juice? With that hair I must have resembled a picked chicken.

"Is your mamma home?"

"Yes," I said, holding down my hair with both hands.

"Can you go get her? I got only two corn-fed chickens left. Fresh-dressed this morning. I got a few brown eggs on the truck too."

"Just a minute," I said and went to get my mother. I thought, This boy doesn't go to our school, I won't have to see him, what do I care. I wondered why they wore white shirts when white was the hardest to keep clean. Was he Folami and Akin's brother? Because by then I knew that all of the Reds were Quanders, and few of them ever went to our schools.

At first my curiosity about Obadele, Folami, and Akin was casual. Other matters concerned me more. For instance, why

I had never heard about squaring a corner until my turn in the tryouts for the Drill Team. Why, after a month of school, no boy except the doofus Alvin Kidd had ever called me up. And the school's upcoming speech competition. The way I saw it, the competition was the only imminent thing whose outcome I could influence in the least. I hoped that Mrs. Welche, our new white teacher, would select me to represent our class.

Mrs. Welche had made *The Kansan* the spring before with her insistence that as an exercise "for all involved," she and one of our English teachers at Douglass should exchange schools. It would be a "first." At that point we had two white students at Douglass and no white teachers. The two students were sisters who had come by choice and with much fanfare. A reluctant superintendent had made it clear that a few more years would pass before the new desegregation law would take effect districtwide.

But Mrs. Welche was having none of it. At one time her husband had been a member of the Board of Education, and people said she must have known something damaging to hold over the superintendent's head. People said the school would go to pot, that there would be no discipline with a white woman coming in and changing the rules. Others thought it was a show of good faith.

I didn't mind that she had come. Her blue eyes and brown hair didn't seem to matter to anybody, and I was flattered by the fact that she noticed my small talent for public speaking. I liked her even more when she suggested I learn "Annabel Lee" by Edgar Allan Poe, and represent our class in the competition.

Wanda was a convenient, if reluctant, practice audience.

Her mother, eager for Wanda's interest in anything other than her "Annie Had a Baby" record, encouraged me to come and recite for them some evenings. And one of those evenings she brought out a slim volume of poems called *God's Trombones*.

"This belongs to Reverend's wife," she said. "It's a nice book, but Wanda isn't ever going to make use of it." She said that if I wanted I could keep it for a while.

I took the book home. The more I read, the more excited I became about the poems. They reminded me of spirituals. I wouldn't have been surprised to find that Reverend had borrowed some of these lines to use in his sermons. Any one of these poems was sure to make an audience sit up and take notice.

"If you really feel that strongly about it," Mrs. Welche said, "then I'm willing to let you switch. Choose one poem and we'll see how it goes."

> *And God stepped out on space,*
> *And He looked around and said:*
> *I'm lonely—I'll make Me a world.*

That was it. "The Creation." I was set.

"We'll try it tomorrow after school," Mrs. Welche said.

PERHAPS I THOUGHT Folami would make an exotic critic. True, I wanted her to hear my recitation, but that wasn't all. I was curious. She had attracted me and everyone else precisely because of our superstition, based on hearsay, that she had powers. Her face was no different from any of our faces— moon-round, dark as Karo syrup, with big black eyes, nothing unusual. She was a little stout, but she didn't have to worry, Red Quander women never wore store-bought clothes. We all wondered why they made no effort at being stylish.

"Don't you feel funny being the only girl with wraparound skirts down to your ankles?" I asked her.

"It's all I've ever worn. All of my friends at home wear them too, you all just don't get to see them."

"But your skirts are too straight, you can't walk that good, let alone run in them."

"Yes I can," she said.

I didn't know how to ask her about those sloppy-looking blouses that didn't match the skirts. Why didn't they wear them tucked in? And what kind of hairstyle was up under that gèle?

We had physical education, English, and algebra together. Wanda claimed that Folami smelled, but that was after Folami showed us the stone she rubbed under her arms instead of using baking soda or Mum.

"You're smelling your upper lip," I told Wanda. "I'm around her a lot and I never smell anything."

"Well, she doesn't ever take showers after gym."

"At her house they probably still have to heat water for a bath. Maybe she isn't ready for showers. She always looks clean."

Folami was careful always to slip into her one-piece gym suit beneath her long skirt, then go through contortions getting the top part on under her long-sleeved blouses, all the while holding on to her gèle. And after gym she reversed the careful plan so that no one would ever see any part of her without clothes, except of course her arms and legs. We all hated the common shower too. Granted, the rest of us didn't have to worry about headwraps, but we couldn't afford to get *our* hair wet either. We managed by putting on shower caps and running through. I thought Folami was silly to risk getting an F for the semester just because she was modest. Anyhow, I couldn't reconcile her modesty with her powers. Finally, though, Folami stopped getting dressed at all for gym, and when we suited up, she went to Study Hall with the girls who were on their periods.

"Why don't you ever suit up anymore?" I asked her.

"Too much trouble," she said.

I thought about those hideous scars on the bodies of young African girls pictured in the encyclopedia.

"It's only twice a week," I said. "Why don't you take your gym suit home every day and wear it to school under your dress?"

She didn't seem moved by my idea, but she thanked me. No one else had bothered to notice her problem.

I wouldn't say we were friends after that, but we were okay. Since Wanda usually talked to, walked with, or hid from some boy every morning, Folami and I began meeting on the corner in front of Doll's Market to walk to school. Generally she had little to say, but she waited there each morning with her brother—Akin of the white shirt and flimsy brown trousers. I never saw either of them eating in the cafeteria, yet every morning they had delicious-smelling, paper-wrapped lunches that disappeared before they walked to Redtown in the evening.

I knew in my heart that Folami didn't want to bring me home with her. I considered myself clever enough, though, to talk her into it.

"That's okay, my mother is a little peculiar too," I told her.

And when she mentioned dinner, I told her, "Don't worry about that. I'll wait until I go home to eat dinner."

"How long is this poem?" she asked me. I assured her that it wouldn't take more than five or ten minutes. I didn't want her to think I was going to bore her with some dry speech.

"Are you sure you want to hear me do my poem?" I said. I didn't think that she would refuse me. She told me that it was usually the old people who recited things to them in Redtown. I let her know that I wouldn't be too embarrassed if somebody else listened.

And so, for the first time, I went to Redtown and into a Red Quander house. What was so different there? The strangely heady, earth-oil smell. The glow from a kerosene lamp. The cloth on the wall, the circle of chairs. The shiny coal of an old woman, her skinny white braids sprouting like a fringe from her red gèle. The carved stool in the corner of the first room where she sat. The snuff she packed into her lower lip. The second room and the low table with no chairs. Akin in gray overalls. And Folami's mother, with a figure and a gèle fuller and more regal than Folami's.

"Who is this girl?" her mother asked Folami.

Folami answered that I was a friend who had helped her at school.

"What is she doing here?"

"I'm helping her learn a poem."

"Hi, Mrs. Quander," I said.

At that greeting she flashed a mouthful of square white teeth, then burst out with laughter so deep that at first I started to laugh too. Softening it a bit, she shook her head and went back to the kitchen.

Akin brought a plate of strange candy. "Crystal ginger," Folami said. "Take one, it's good. It's rolled in sugar."

Folami sat down in the first room on one of the wooden, straight-back chairs. I stood before her.

> *And as far as the eye of God could see,*
> *Darkness covered everything . . .*

"Wait," Folami said. "You look dead. You ought to move around. When we tell stories, we move our arms and look at people. We make faces and jump around. Don't just stand there. *Do* something!

> *And the light that was left from making the sun*
> *God gathered it up in a shining ball*
> *And flung it against the darkness,*
> *Spangling the night with the moon and stars.*

When Folami's mother came to sit and listen, I hesitated.

"Keep going. Suppose somebody at school walks in while you're up there. Are you going to stop?" Folami asked.

> *Then down between*
> *The darkness and the light*
> *He hurled the world;*
> *Then He stopped and looked and saw*
> *That the earth was hot and barren.*
> *So God stepped over to the edge of the world*
> *And He spat out the seven seas—*

Another woman, stout and wearing a robe affair, came walking from the kitchen through the eating room to stand outside the circle of chairs and listen. Then still another woman. Then a girl about Folami's age entered, and they sat in the circle of chairs.

> *And the waters above the earth came down,*
> *The cooling waters came down.*

They held themselves, listening intently, rocked and looked at the floor. Now and again someone hummed. When finally I finished, they were quiet.

"They tell you this story at school?" Folami's mother asked, casually.

"Irene is going to say this poem in front of the whole school," Folami said.

"You like this story too?" her mother asked Folami.

"It's just a poem out of a book. It doesn't mean anything," Folami said.

Her mother stood abruptly, and pointed a long finger nearly touching my chest. "Don't come back here to our place with stories," she said. "When you talk, you talk to them that understands you. Not us."

Immediately I was out the door. And there he was, the boy with the chickens. The lean, smooth boy, taller this time, white teeth, ripe lips, sloe eyes.

"Scared you, didn't she?" he said. I ignored him. He walked at my heels, teasing.

"What you scared of, somebody gonna sprinkle dust? Take some of your hair? Turn you into a dog? Guess you won't be coming around here singing your sweet little songs."

That broke the spell. I surely wasn't going to let some boy, Red Quander or not, make fun of me.

"If you have the nerve to come over to Tenth Street trying to sell those puny guinea hens and sorry brown eggs, I can come over in Redtown to see my friend."

"What you mean guineas? Your mother sure doesn't mind giving me a dollar every Saturday."

I turned around and looked at him. "Those women in there would just as soon bawl me out as look at me. At least my mother is nice to you."

That caught him off guard.

"What was that you were telling them, anyway?" he asked.

"It was a poem I have to memorize for school."

"Oh. Well, you better be careful about what you do in Redtown, especially in that house," he said, and he smiled. "My name is Obadele."

Every Saturday my mother bought her usual chickens and eggs and teased with Wanda about our Red Quander eggman. She watched me, though. By the way I washed and braided my hair late Friday nights to get up straightening it early Saturdays before Dele came with the eggs, she knew. She knew by the school clothes I put on just to have on. I was at least fascinated.

"Who's that egg boy and how you know them Red Quanders?" she asked me.

"I've been to one of their houses," I said. "And his name is Obadele Quander. He's some kin to Folami, the one who goes to our school."

"I see he got a funny name too, but you know all of them is Quanders. Every last one of them."

"That's just like us. All of us are Wilsons."

"In *this* house," my mother said. "Not in the whole city. Don't make no sense one man having so many women. You stay away from there."

I saw Folami every day at school. She was apologetic about her mother's ways, but until I pressed her, she didn't say any more.

"Who is your father?" I asked.

"His name is Oba Quander," she said. "Why?"

"I don't know. Curious, I guess. And what's your mother's name?"

She told me that her mother had died when she and Akin were born, but the woman I saw—her Mamma Mandisa—had raised them. Those other women were all sort of aunts of hers.

No mystery there. I thought about the play aunt I once had. I told Folami what my mother had said about their unusual ways, especially about how men could have several wives. She said it was true, but she said, "So what? To us every father is Oba—that means king. We're just a family that keeps to itself. Only bigger."

I didn't quite get it. If so many had the same father and every father had the same name, how would I know one Oba Quander from another?

"*You* wouldn't," she said. "*I* would."

The evening Obadele first walked with Folami, Akin, and me down by the creek, he itched to tell me how pure the Quanders were, how, across generations, their blood had seldom been mixed.

"Who cares?" I said. "Besides, lots of people say that, but how do you know?"

"I know because I'm my father's son, and my father came

from his pure-blooded father, and we go on back just like that to the time we were first brought here. Same is true with my mother."

"Why don't you speak African, then? You all sound just like us to me. Like you're from around here."

"I do, a little," he said. "Anyway, we can use the same words you use, but it doesn't mean we speak the same language. We don't want to be like you," he said.

"Well, you sure do go through a lot of trouble trying to be different," I said.

"Us? What about you? You can't be what you really are at your school," Obadele said.

"I knew you'd say that, but it's not true." I tried to sell him on the advantages of common knowledge, but he wasn't interested.

"Look," he said. And he untied his red satin. I think I expected a conk because the red cloth fit his head as closely as the do-rags my father sometimes wore. I wasn't prepared for the way Dele's naps grew in perfect swirls around his head, like a cap.

He said to me, "Cut off all your hair and let it be, then see what happens. I dare you."

No wonder Folami had held on to her gèle at school. Was he crazy? The last thing I wanted was hair shorter than mine already was. Who wanted to look like an African, even a civilized one?

I didn't want to look like him, but I wouldn't have minded having his gift for storytelling. He knew he was good.

"This is the way it was," he would say. And then he would become quiet as if he were recalling all the details of a life he once knew. This set a certain mood. Then he would begin:

"At first there was no solid land. There were only two kingdoms. There was the sky, the domain of the *orisha* Olorun, the Sky God. And far below that, the watery mists, the domain of Olukun, a female *orisha*. The two kingdoms existed separately, and they let each other alone. Back then, all of life was in the sky, where Olorun lived with many other powerful *orishas*.

"There was Ifa, who could see the future and who was in charge of Fate; Eshu, who was made of chance and whim, and who causes the unforeseen troubles and pleasures in our lives. There was Agemo, the chameleon, and many others, but the most important was Obatala, the Sky God's son."

Obadele went on to tell how it was Obatala who formed the earth. How he hooked a gold chain onto the edge of the sky and descended to the water below, carrying with him a snail's shell filled with sand, a pouch of palm nuts, and the egg that contained the essence of all the *orishas*. The story explained how, when he reached the end of the golden chain, Obatala poured out the sand and dropped the egg, releasing an exquisite bird who scattered the sand, along with the traits of the *orishas*, throughout the mists. In this way he created solid land with hills and valleys. And when he planted his palm nuts, vegetation sprang up on all the earth. Then he saw a reflection of himself in a shallow pool, and began to make figures from the clay, human figures imbued with the personalities of all the *orishas*. He made them carefully and set them in the sun to dry while he quenched his thirst on palm wine. When he resumed his work, because he was intoxicated he made mistakes—the disfigured, the blind, the lame, the deaf. Then the Sky God's breath set the earth spinning, and washed across the figures drying in the sun, bringing them to life. One by one, they rose from the earth and began to do all the things people do. And Obatala, the Sky God's son, became the chief of all the earth.

But every so often, the *orisha* of the watery mists casts powerful juju on the earth, which once was her domain.

I liked Obadele's story, but I was even more fascinated with his version of the mystery of Folami and Akin and their Mamma Mandisa. According to Dele, the twins were not ordinary people. All twins, he said, have the power to bring good fortune into the lives of those who treat them well. Whatever they want, they get. The wise do everything they can to make twins happy.

Obadele said that Akin, the second born, sent Folami into the world first to see if life was worth living. Their mother was suffering great pains at that moment and Folami made this known to Akin. A whole day later, the reluctant Akin arrived, and sure enough, their mother died.

Mandisa was another of their father's wives. Apparently she was always a mean woman. Dele said only that she "used to be troublesome." At any rate, she was hard to get along with and she made an enemy of a neighbor woman, inviting that other woman's juju. And powerful it was. The woman, whose name Dele would not say, caused what he called an *abiku* child to enter Mandisa's womb. This was a child that was born over and over again, a child that died shortly after each birth just to torment Mandisa. But Mandisa was more clever. She took the newborn twins into her house and succeeded in nullifying all of the obeah woman's power.

Week after week, Dele mesmerized me with stories of *orishas*, of lost kingdoms and ancient rulers, and of people—Hausas and Zulus—he claimed I had to thank for more than my black skin. Squat on his haunches on the bank of the creek, he talked about how his father's father's father was the end-all, be-all keeper of the secrets of life, how the old man could recite, for days, every event since the beginning of time without one mistaken word. I was convinced that at least *he* believed what he was saying.

And when Folami gave me an amulet, I pinned it to my brassiere. For an unbeliever, an amulet has no charm. But I liked the idea of it, and maybe it worked because a certain kind of luck followed me to school, right to the stage of our auditorium. Whoever won the competition would represent Douglass in the state competition at KU that next month. Thanks to Mrs. Welche, it was the first year our school would participate. The reading, a kind of oratorical talent show, would be judged by several teachers.

I had decided to wear my navy blue chemise dress with the white collar because I would be standing, and it would show off what I hoped was my slinky-but-not-skinny figure. On the stage, we sat facing the student body and the scattered teacher-judges with their tablets and pens poised. According to their lottery, I was to go third. The Girls' Ensemble sang two selections, we were introduced, and the contest was on.

First the one white student who was competing, Ann Marie Cooper, walked to the podium. I was immediately struck by how confident she seemed. She threw her golden hair back over her shoulder and said good morning to the audience, then turned to greet her fellow schoolmates on the stage. Though brief, her background comments, in which she explained why she had chosen the Gettysburg Address, were more successful than her overheated rendition of Lincoln's speech. I was heartened, but also frustrated. I had not prepared an introduction. Were we expected to follow her example?

John Goodson went next. He towered over the podium. He clutched it, preacher-like, rolled up on the balls of his feet, and in his sonorous best, all but shook the place. *Out of the night that covers me, Black as the Pit from pole to pole!* The assembly sat entirely still. Not once did John let up until he had built to the final *I am the master of my fate; I am the captain of my soul!* with such power that half the students jumped to their feet in applause. Well, okay, I hadn't prepared a nice introduction to put everybody at ease. And "The Creation" certainly couldn't begin on a loud note.

When I stood up, I smoothed the lap creases of my dress and walked deliberately to the podium. I felt the sweat on my palms. Despite my three-inch, pointed-toe shoes, I was short. Nevertheless, in a sudden inspired moment I stepped to the side of the podium and gently opened my arms. Unhurried, I looked from one side of the auditorium to the other, then began. *And God stepped out on space, and He looked around and said: I'm lonely—I'll make Me a world.* I swept out an arm. *And as far as the eye of God could see, darkness covered everything, blacker,* I said "blacker" with a rasp: *. . . blacker than a hundred midnights down in a cypress swamp.* I paused, dropped my arms, turned my head away from the audience, and walked a few steps across the stage. I faced them again, loosely folded my hands in a prayer stance and smiled, nodding my head. *Then God smiled, and the light broke, and the darkness rolled up on one side . . .* and when I said "rolled up," I sang the O sound and made grand loops in the air with one hand, then finished: *. . . and the light stood shining on the other.* I sang "shining" and flung up my other hand. With my entire being bent on heaven, the rest was automatic. *And God said: That's good!*

Some other, bolder Irene had taken over, and batted her eyes hard when she came to *batted His eyes and the lightning flashed* . . . and she clapped the thunder and toiled with her hands until anyone watching would be hard put to deny that she held an actual lump of clay. As that Irene *blew into it the breath of life* . . . six hundred souls in the auditorium held their breath, quiet, until Mr. Harris's "Amen!" released them to clap hard and long.

Donald South closed with Tennyson's "Ulysses," potentially a good choice, since the last line, *To strive, to seek, to find, and not to yield*, had been selected for the senior class motto. Unfortunately for Donald, that fact contributed to his undoing when several seniors shouted out the line a beat ahead of him, destroying his delivery of the final words.

I won. Obadele was not impressed. What was the point? What did it mean to win? So I could recite a poem—was it an important poem? Why would I want to do that for a school that taught me nothing relevant? Why was I so bent on impressing a white woman teacher?

He's jealous, I thought. I realized that in some ways he was smarter than he knew. He could discuss a simple story with a depth no one in my class would attempt. The Red Quander men and women mainly taught their children at home. I suppose they had books to augment all of that reciting the old folks did. But wasn't I the one who watched John Cameron Swayze explain the world several times a week on our new television, something Dele could see only if he dared to take his Red Quander self into the Montgomery Ward store on the avenue? Didn't I know the facts he dismissed outright about the girl ironically named Brown who lived in Topeka, just fifty miles away, and who had been named in the Supreme Court case that was changing everything? Ours was the school that had maps and literature. Mine was the mother who saw to it that I went there every day. I knew more facts. He was jealous. I knew more.

The next time he knew more. He knew that if he carried a load of chicken wire and rags in his Oba-fixed truck, the state patrol would not stop a Red Quander riding out in the county on a Friday night. He knew the place in the hills at Wyandotte Lake where, if you stood on the edge of a boulder, you could see the whole of the winding water. He knew that the moon affects everything it shines on. He knew that I was afraid to be with him and the dark trees, and how a scent is a charm, how the nose can catch what the eye misses. He was the one who explained the rot of Skagg Creek as something to get beyond. That in it I could discover the wonder of everything turning to dust, and my hunger for the smell of earth's dark life. Obadele knew the effect that smell would have on me as he oiled it into his pores.

I had never talked the talk for hours on the telephone with him, never drank a single Nehi with him at Nettie's Dinette. He had never been past the front door of my house, or seen me dressed up at church, never even heard of Al Hibbler and "Unchained Melody." We had never slow-danced.

"It's all right," he said. Inside his truck, on a bed of soft rags, we took off our clothes. Without light to see by, he touched me as if, slowly and gently, he were shaping my body into a woman. He opened door after door. This was the slow-dance I had wanted to learn. I found the steps awkward, but he was a born dancer. Instinctively, he set a rhythm and unchained us both.

FOR SOMEONE WHO loved school, I became a slouch. I ignored poetry and logarithms. My mind busied itself with logistics. Meeting Dele. At first it didn't matter that he had no telephone, I saw him every morning and every evening unless he had to go hauling or selling in his father's truck too early and too late. Or unless Mrs. Welche pressed me about staying after school to practice my speech. Or unless Folami stuck to me like warm mush and asked too many questions, unless Akin spied, unless Wanda used her sixth sense.

"Hope you know you can get pregnant," Wanda said. "Red Quanders don't play. They'll be workin hoodoo on you, and you won't even know it."

Then it mattered that he had no phone. Even when I came early and stayed late, I couldn't be sure he would be under the trestle. He said that people like us who were forced to hide had to be careful. We were to act as if nothing had changed. But it was impossible. I lived to see Dele, and looked for him every chance I got, despite his father and my schedule and my friends. I didn't care what time I got home, or what time I got to school.

Once, I even met him after the morning classes had already begun. The crisp November air was filled with him. In the truck we drove right past the school, out to the highway and up through Olathe. To Leavenworth to see anything we had never seen, which turned out to be the prison and the army base. I wished for a gèle and long skirt so that people could see that we belonged together.

"It's more than the clothes," Dele said. "You have to *be* one of us, or at least see yourself as we do."

"Who knows," I told him, "maybe someday I will."

As we rode out Highway 40, the designation "great" came easily to my mind when I looked at the plains. Fields of winter wheat, undulant and green, surged to recede into pale seas of corn, or plowed black acreage, or loam as brown as the bread it supported. It seemed that if we could rise high enough above those vast stretches, we would see that they formed the very center of a continent. And if we focused closely, a certain symmetry would emerge with our highway as the dividing line, and a boy who was Obadele and a girl who was my very self as the axis from which it all sprang.

We drove on to Topeka that afternoon, licking his salt fish from our fingers. I wanted to show him the streets where history had begun to unfold.

"It isn't going to make any difference," Dele said. "White people don't want you all in their schools, and no court can change that. You should keep to your own, forget about them."

He didn't understand, but I was in no mood to spoil our adventure. When we got home, I saw no reason for him to drop me off anywhere but in front of my house. Of course I didn't expect to see my mother watching for me out the front door. My mother was never tempted to mince words. I knew what was coming when she yelled, "Just a minute," and came out to the truck.

"I know what you're doing and I'm not going to allow it," she said to Dele. "Irene is not one of y'all and I don't want her around y'all. Don't make me come over to Redtown looking for your people, because that's just what I'm going to do if I catch you around here again. You can consider that a promise," she told Dele.

"You can't do that!" I said.

"Don't try me, Irene. Get your hind parts out of that truck."

Given my opinion on how little my mother knew about love, I was furious. As soon as Dele left I told her I loved him. "I'm not going to stop just because you don't understand him."

She attempted to pull rank with "You ain't too grown yet for me to whip."

"I don't care," I told her. "You can't stop me."

"I can tell your daddy," she said. She was losing ground.

"I don't care. Tell him."

My love for a Red Quander had made me my own woman.

LATER THAT SAME week, I missed seeing Folami and noted that she had been absent for several days. I asked Dele about her.

"I don't know. I'm not her keeper," he said. "Maybe she's had enough of y'all's school."

And I asked Akin about her.

"She's at home," he said.

"What's the matter with her?"

"Nothing," Akin said. "She's just not coming back to school anymore."

At the first glimmer of a realization, it's hard to distinguish titillation from dread. I wondered if Folami's absence had anything to do with Obadele and me. Friday of that week my mother and I stood in the door waving Wanda on, when who else but Dele rode by in his truck. I remember clearly that it was a Friday evening because I had decided against going to the football game with Wanda.

Since the confrontation with my mother, Dele had made me promise that we would be more careful. Although I had missed him under the trestle that morning, I was shocked that he would provoke my mother by coming to our street, and thrilled that he would defy her to see me. His truck didn't stop, though. Just rattled on by.

"He can drive on any street he wants to," my mother said. "It's a free country. But he better not be looking for you." She had already heard me tell Wanda that I wasn't going to the game, and so I couldn't get out to talk to him that night.

Wanda did, however. First thing Saturday morning she came over to get me.

"Come on, we got to walk to the store. Mamma needs some milk," she said. Wanda never got up early on Saturday mornings. I hurried to finish curling my hair, just in case. Once we were outside my house, walking fast, our breath disappearing in the fog, I urged her, "Tell me what's up."

"Nothing, why?"

"I know something is up. Your mother probably doesn't even know you're out of bed."

"Okay, I just want us to talk," Wanda said.

"About what? Did you see Dele last night? Did he ask you to get me out of the house this morning?"

"Yeah, I saw him last night. Let's go over to my house. It's too cold out here."

Appeal moved toward alarm. I dismissed the fantasy of seeing the truck in the alley behind her house and went quickly with her up to her attic bedroom.

"Sit down," she said. I sat down. She looked out her window and shook her head. Then she sat down beside me and surrendered.

"You know Folami, right?

"Yeah."

"Well, she's pregnant."

"What?"

"Yeah," Wanda said, letting it register.

"So that's why she can't come back to school. How did you find out?"

"How do you think? Obadele told me."

"I just asked him—why would he tell *you?*" My stomach began to float up.

"So I could tell you what he didn't have the guts to tell you himself. He's about to become a little king in Redtown. Full-fledged man. No more nigger girls."

I didn't want to hear any more from Wanda.

"Look, don't blame me," she said. "I wasn't there to hold the light while he did it to her. I just told him I'd tell you."

I understood the words, but it didn't make sense to me. There had to be something Wanda missed. That, or Obadele must have told Wanda a half-truth because of the pressure from the world.

It took a Monday morning under the trestle waiting in the cold, and a Monday afternoon in gym class hearing about Folami, and a Monday evening walking around outside Redtown with Wanda, hoping to see Dele's truck—it took all that for me to allow that it could even be possible. On Wednesday, after Wanda left me under the trestle in the cold morning, cursed me out in the evening, and threatened to go get my mother, I was only slightly more convinced that Dele could have done this.

By Friday it became clear that it would take a lot more than Wanda's word or my mother's threats to bring the fullness of it home. Why go to school when what I needed to know was in Redtown? I fastened my car coat, tied my scarf, collected my books, and left the house.

So what if I didn't have the slightest clue to where Dele lived? I would look for the truck.

Instead, when I got to Redtown, I headed for the only familiar place, Folami's house. My father used to say, when somebody burns down a house, he can't hide the smoke. I had to see her with my own eyes first. As I tramped up to the door, her Mamma Mandisa opened it, filling the doorway, hands on her hips, superiority beaming on her face.

"What you want, girl?"

"Can I speak to Folami?"

"Nothing around here for you. She's not coming back to the school, so you may as well get on away from here." She didn't wait for me to respond before she closed the door.

I found the truck parked in front of a house covered in brown tar-paper siding. I knocked loudly on the front door. When that didn't rouse anyone, I knocked again, with both fists, and when that didn't do it, I went to the back of the house and knocked on the door with my feet. When that didn't bring Dele outside to tell me that I had it all wrong, I got into the truck and laid on the horn. Surely he would hear, surely he would see me sitting out there. The horn blasted a minute or two, then gave up in a hoarse bleat. I got out of the truck, with its cracked window and wrong-color fender and its smell of kerosene and earth.

Where could I go? I wanted to be some other place, anywhere except this red town where I was certain that red eyes
watched my foolish misery and cackled their red pleasure. I
followed the railroad tracks, where I could be lost without
losing my way.

For hours I walked. Through the woods, outside other
neighborhoods, along the river, and into the outskirts of Rattlebone. I was one with the fallow fields I passed through, and
with the harvested ones too, where sheaves stood like empty
spools. How could he? How could this be happening to me?

I got home after dark that night. Through the window in
the front door I could see the kitchen and Wanda at the table
with my mother and father, chattering to distract them. I
could have been a ghost the way my mother flinched when
she saw me.

Wanda said, "Girl, we were really worried—weren't we,
Miss Wilson?" I knew it was her attempt to diffuse the tight-
ness in the air.

"You ain't got no business wandering around by yourself
this late," my father said. "I was waiting till nine. You better
be glad you got some sense and came on home before I had
to come after you." His speech sounded rehearsed.

My mother went to the stove and dipped up a bowl of oxtail
stew. She unbuttoned my car coat for me and touched her
fingers to my cheek.

"Too cold for you to be out with nothing on," she said.
"Sit down and eat." I obeyed.

Days later, Wanda broached the subject again. "Welcome
to the club," she said. "I could have told you. They're all
alike. Dogs, all of them. Forget him. You have to tell yourself

nothing happened. Nothing at all happened. After all," she said, "I'm the only one at school who knows the whole story, and I know how to keep it to myself. There's nothing else to do unless you plan to jump in the river."

I tried following Wanda's expert advice, act as if nothing had happened. Forget Obadele Quander. He wasn't anyone, anyway. If my life was going to be a mess, it wasn't going to show.

I HAD MISSED several rehearsals with Mrs. Welche. I frightened myself with the possibility that I had ruined my chances for the competition.

"I understand you've been having some problems at home," she said. I wondered who she had been talking to.

"I hope whatever is going on, you won't miss any more days of school or we may have to reconsider the tournament," she said.

That short-circuited my cure. What I needed now was a victory. Mrs. Welche was offering that possibility, and I would focus all my energy on claiming it.

"I'm fine now," I said. I wanted to give the right slant to what she had heard. "I won't have to miss any more days of school."

"You know," she said, "those students of ours that live in Redtown, from what I understand, you've been spending a lot of time with them. I'm not so sure they're the kind of influence you should be exposed to. Most of them aren't even interested in school."

"Yes, ma'am, I know," I said. I could not look at her.

"They have strange ideas," she said.

"Yes, ma'am," I said.

"They don't believe in God, and they don't believe in washing themselves," she said.

I didn't say anything.

"They're all related, yet they marry each other."

"I'm having a little trouble with the last part of my introduction," I said.

The tournament was to be held on the Saturday after Thanksgiving. Mrs. Welche had already arranged for me to ride with her and a student from her old school. Of the twenty-five contestants, I suspected, few to none would look like me. I considered it an initiation into the world I would move through if and when I went to college.

Usually I rehearsed twice a week in the auditorium after school with Mrs. Welche sitting at various places to see how well I projected. Occasionally another teacher would sit in, or a student would sneak in to watch. About ten days before Thanksgiving, Mrs. Welche asked me to meet her in her classroom instead of going to the auditorium. When I got there she sat on her desk with her arms folded.

"I received some bad news a couple of days ago," she said. "I've been wondering how to tell you. Why don't you sit down."

She picked up the letter from her desk. "I want you to know that if I had known this, I would have never even mentioned the state competition to you. I've been involved with it for years. I just didn't think."

She was looking at the letter, but of course, I already knew.

"They won't let me be in it, will they?" I said.

"I'm sorry," she said. "The contest has never been open to you all. They say in the future . . ."

"But isn't that against the law now?"

"Well, sort of," she said. "But things take time."

This was not news. I told myself that perhaps it had happened this way for a good reason. Maybe I would have frozen up on that stage. Those people probably had never even heard of James Weldon Johnson. From the way Mrs. Welche had responded at first, I believed she had never heard of him herself.

Then Mrs. Welche said, "I was just thinking, you've done all this work for nothing. Wouldn't it be wonderful if we could salvage some of it, put it to good use?"

"Yes, but how?" I asked her.

"Well, you know, Ann Marie Cooper is a pretty good speaker. She has poise and she can project. I had her read "The Creation" for me yesterday, and she wasn't nearly as good as you are, but she could probably learn to do it your way. I thought if you would teach it to her, you know, teach her your inflections and gestures, all the drama you put into it, she could take it to state."

I gathered my books without answering. Outside, November trees had lost their leaves, and their branches showed crooked against the clouds. I took the shortcut along the tracks past Redtown. Without looking down, I crossed the narrow trestle and went home.

A SUNDAY
KIND OF
LOVE

Take me to the water. Take me to the water, to be baptized.
Thomas Pemberton gets the song going in his head and keeps
the tempo by tapping with his fingers on the stove top. He
waits at Wanda Coles's place, watches while she takes her
time getting ready to go with him to church. Her dress, blue
and silky, is still unzipped to a long V down her ginger-pale
back. He notices that she hasn't put on a brassiere. The image
of old people flashes in his mind—folks old as he is now—
swaying straggly on the banks of Hobbs Creek, singing about
being baptized. Those same sanctimonious eyes will watch this
young-girl-of-a-woman strut with him into church.

"Don't lean against the stove, Thomas, you'll mess up your
suit," Wanda says. "Do me a favor, why don't you. Fold up
the bed and sit down while I get myself together."

Thomas folds the bed into a sofa, but instead of sitting, he
walks around, absently touching things. Pulls a dried leaf from
her sweet potato plant on top the TV. Tests the heart-shaped
magnets stuck to her refrigerator door.

"I don't think I ever said so before," he says, "but I never
really got baptized."

"So? You think they gonna dredge that up?" Wanda piddles in her closet and he wishes she would hurry.

"Naw, I was just thinking. I was ten. You couldn't go in unless you were at least ten. Down at the creek, when it came time for the preacher to dip me under—he'd done already blessed me and had his hand over my face—I went to fighting and carrying on trying to catch my breath. I hooped and hollered so, they said I got happy and let me go. You should have seen me scrambling for the bank."

Wanda chuckles. December sleet crackles static on the windows and she complains that her straw hat with the blue flowers won't do for wintertime, not with her mother's old Persian lamb, and how she needs the hat for the dress to look churchy.

"I guess you'll be wearing something up under that dress."

"I wouldn't be going to church half-naked," she says. "Soon as I find something decent to wear, the weather messes up." She sticks a black pillbox too far down on her head.

"What you think?"

He is thinking that she needs some other kind of dress to wear, shoes with the heels and toes in. She's twenty and she looks it, too young. Too slender. He sees them entering together, sees his own heaviness in the buttoned suit coat. Before his hair thinned on top, he could have passed for forty. He pulls at the hairs in the mole on his chin. He needs a pair of scissors.

"I guess it's all right, but why don't you stay home, Wanda?"

"Why? What you think is going to happen?"

She's getting started again. How does *he* know? He shrugs. She continues to regard the inside of her closet like a place she's never seen before.

A Sunday Kind of Love

"I'm in this with you, Thomas, but if I ever felt glad about not belonging to your church, today is the day. And you know what? God himself couldn't be as worked up about this as those people at your church."

"Stay here, Wanda. Everybody's going to be looking, you know that. Why you need to see who they are? Why they need to see you? You don't belong to the church, so they can't do nothing to you."

"What about this?" she says, holding up a black dress with a sequined top.

"Don't ask me. Wear anything you want to put on," he says. "What do I know about your dresses? You don't half listen to me no way."

"Well, I didn't know you had to be a dressmaker to decide on what looks like church. I *am* talking to the king of the deacons, right? Don't sweat it, Thomas. I should have gone on down to Osawatomie and seen Puddin this morning instead of fooling around with you. I ought to just keep my behind right here and leave you hanging."

She yanks something off the rod in the closet, something from the pile on the chair, from under the sofa, from a drawer, off a hanger on the doorknob. She zips herself into blue shantung, cocks an orange-feathered felt hat on the side of her head, clamps rhinestones to her ears, slings her Persian lamb around her shoulders, marches out her kitchenette's private-entrance door down to the silver-sleeted sidewalk, and situates herself in the passenger seat of Thomas's car.

Behind her, Thomas shuffles along, overcoat hanging on his arm. He climbs into the driver's side and fishtails his dated Buick down the street. Eventually he slows down.

"What you so mad about?"

"I ain't mad, I just can't see why you so bent on me not going. It ain't like you couldn't use the company."

He touches her hand on the seat. "I don't care 'bout them people."

"I know that, Thomas. I didn't say you was scared, I just want to be there. What's wrong with that?"

"Well, you know you can't sit with me, don't you? I'm sitting up front with the deacons."

Wanda moves her hand. "I been inside a church before, Thomas. I know where the deacons sit."

He knows for sure she can read the part of him that wants her there. During the first year after his wife, Lydia, passed, he seldom said more than "How do" to anyone. Yet every so often Wanda would stop by his big empty rooming house with a newspaper under her arm and make him a cup of Lipton's before she went home to her new place next door. Even for months after that, she sat with him as he picked over plates of food she had brought. She started him playing dominoes again. Being nice to an old man. At the time, he knew her only as one of the neighborhood kids grown up, a closer neighbor since the Scotts next door started taking in roomers. She was the retarded boy, Puddin's, sister. Thaddeus and Wilma Coles's child come into womanhood. Not that far past being a spring chicken, she had someday notions about a supper club she would own, fame that would find her singing.

As the choir marches in on "Highway to Heaven," Wanda and a few others come into the sanctuary through two sets of swinging doors. Thomas sits with the other deacons, three of them on either side of the pulpit facing each other. From where he sits he can see the mural behind the piano, the baptized Jesus with a dove descending. Afraid that Wanda will sit in his line of vision and thus invite every eye to see if and how he looks at her, Thomas makes the slightest adjustment to his round-back deacon's chair. He senses her taking a seat, crossing her legs. He feels her rhinestone presence near the back. *Take me to the water.*

Most Sundays he anticipates the steady build from the stuffiness of opening hymns and announcements through the familiar gospel numbers and on to the pitch Reverend reaches as he gets into the sermon. But today the service lags. Second Sunday, Young People's Day. Junior ushers. Girls in their black skirts and white blouses, preening and chewing gum. Looking at the boys. Forgetting that they are on duty. Missing their cues. Doors swing open when Reverend is in the middle of prayer. People find their own seats. Second Sunday.

Thomas sits still through the first anthem. Another begins. If he moves his things—hymnal, notepad, Bible—from beside his chair and onto his lap, he might call attention to himself. He picks up the white Bible, unzips it, and opens it to any scripture. Something to do. He never liked hosanna music. When he thinks "church music," he thinks music-by-ear. Soul-showing music. Alive. With anthems, the choir has to know each note by name. He looks at them now, studying as they go, moving their lips to the two-three-fours in between and never taking their eyes from the page. Spirit hasn't got a chance.

It's too warm. The wool suit prickles against his back and arms. He fidgets, sweats freely, wrings the surprise of it in his hands. He will have to settle down.

He wants to look at his watch. Instead he gets up the nerve to look across the congregation. James Wilson is here. At least one friend. Half of them must have been waiting for this moment. They stare as if he alone sits before them. And they don't look away, either. Even the janitor. So smug. So Sunday clean. They are wrong to judge him, haul him up.

Yet in a way he can see why they would be upset. What really bothers him is this sense of everything and nothing to be said—no words for the kind of thing his mind can't quite grasp, can't quite let go of, either.

All right. Maybe it isn't so complicated. Sure, she was Something Else. Back last summer he thought about Wanda a lot, yes, as a woman. He can admit that. Every day, in fact. She was a welcome relief from the heaviness in his head, the tension in his chest. After a year he had finally begun to come to grips with Lydia having a stroke and dying on him like that. Not giving him a chance to say goodbye.

Wanda told him, "I know about living with yourself when it doesn't seem like you're fit to live period." But he didn't believe she could know. As time went on, she babied him. Told him to let it alone. It wasn't his to understand. Told him God wasn't angry, things like that. Maybe she knew. She'd had to put her brother away. Maybe she knew.

Just as a heartache eases, it happened gradually, over evenings in early summer. In his backyard, sagging low in his web chair, he counted Lydia's zinnias and gladioli in neat tiers against the whitewashed back of the house. More than anything, Lydia had loved her flowers. If she had died in summer, he would have cut all the blossoms in the yard for her bier. She died in the fall, though, when nothing bloomed except his grief.

Wanda came by nearly every evening, wearing her black-and-white Cakebox uniform, taking a shortcut through the alley to her place. She brought him little cake boxes of doughnuts or bear claws from the bakery in the county mall where she worked days. He made a habit of clipping sprigs of baby's breath for her.

Usually at some point in the early evening, when the trees caught the sun's white fire so bright Thomas couldn't look at them, he would turn his chair to face the rooming house next door and sure enough, there Wanda would be, trouncing down her outdoor stairway to the alley, wearing three-inch, some-color pumps and bare, jazz-singing dresses, baby's breath over one ear, on her way to Chez de Maurice's.

"Watch out for the fools, and that includes the smart ones too," he would yell. Wave her on her way. He felt protective; her mother seldom came to see her.

"You ought to go with me to church," he would tease.

"You go to church enough for the whole neighborhood," she would yell back to him.

Time makes habits. Is this the kind of detail he should begin with when he gets up to talk? People can understand that when things change slowly, change doesn't always register. Should he defend himself right away?

Habits ripen. He remembers summer turning rampageous with flowers—wild hollyhocks, tiger lilies—and Wanda again, keeping him company. Religiously, he went to prayer meetings, Bible classes, but no one except Wanda came to sit with him in his web chairs in the backyard and point out how the sun turns trees char-black against the late sky. It became natural that he offered to run her out to Chez de Maurice's in his car, and that she took him up on it. He listened to her no-account-men stories and laughed at the things she said to keep her customers straight at the bakery.

Can they understand how his loss could be embraced by

something fresh, something vital, un-quiet? Should he tell them how if you just keep breathing, you learn to look forward to it again? How a simple idea can bless the past? How one evening Wanda suggested that Lydia was somewhere wishing for all her flowers?

"I used to see her out here all the time, working on her garden."

And the next morning Thomas went out to his yard early. By the time the sun grew warm enough to dry the dew, he had cleared the yard to a neutral green. Queen Anne's lace, zinnias, everything carefully cut. At the cemetery, on the entire length of Lydia's grave, he took special care to arrange the brilliant colors—the orange with the yellow, the sapphire with the purple, vermilion, pink, magenta—so that they dazzled him to tears.

It is difficult to see anything clearly through the church's modern frosted windows, but as Thomas sits listening to the sermon, he can make out the blurred outline of a hand. Outside the window the branch of a small tree ends in a fan of twigs like the skeletal spread of a thumb, a palm, and four fingers. He entertains the thought of the hand of God. Waving. Hand of God? He must be off. He pulls a handkerchief from his back pocket and runs it over his face.

"Blessed be the tie that binds our hearts in Christian love." Reverend speaks the words and the choir breaks into the Benediction. Thomas takes out his pocket watch slowly and steals a quick glance. One-ten. He has been sitting for more than an hour while Reverend preached and he hasn't uttered a single amen, paid practically no attention at all. If he could just stand up and stretch, walk up the aisle and out the door.

He chances a glimpse of Wanda, but she's watching the choir and doesn't see him.

Reverend clears his throat and measures his way through the next speech.

"As most of you know, we're having a general church meeting here in just a little while. Now, this won't be something that the children can take part in, so I want all you womenfolk to take the children downstairs. The junior ushers got cookies and a little something to drink down there. After that, come on back and take your seats. I expect this meeting won't take long. You folks in the choir just leave off your robes and find a seat out here in the sanctuary."

At once the congregation's collective posture undoes itself to a jumble of hats, coats, hands pulling, little legs running. In the stir, Wanda gets up and moves toward the front of the church. Nobody seems to notice. Seeing her, Thomas smiles. She sidesteps into the fourth row and wiggles her fingers hello to him before she sits down. People notice that right away.

And right away, unbidden, a moment overwhelms Thomas's memory—the moment when he fluttered, circled for the lunge into a ginger-colored flame. The evening after a rain, when the sun dropped into the narrow slot between earth and sky. The atmosphere shone with a gold light that turned every blade of green to emerald, any buff to gold long legs coming up the alley, to golden-all-over arms swinging a black-striped cake box, to penny-colored hair feathered around a face, burnished, leaning over his fence into his air, flashing gold-flecked copper eyes, saying, "What you looking at, Thomas?" Laughing. Thomas studies his hands. *Take me to the water.*

Now he's watching from a far distance, or so it seems. Sister

Cotton, sitting with the Ruth Circle, gets up, white taffeta arm in the air.

"I've been knowing Brother Pemberton since he got married over thirty years ago. He's been living without his lovely wife for over two years. It was a shock. He's a man of God. He's come too far and got too close to heaven to turn around now. Whatever he's done, God will forgive him, and we can forgive him too. That's all I got to say."

"Amen." "Amen" rumbled through the congregation.

See. These are his people. They know him. Thomas folds his arms. Reverend should have come himself. Should never have sent the other deacons to talk to Thomas first. This meeting would not be necessary if Reverend had just come to talk to him. Maybe he ought to tell them *that*, show them they had some responsibility in all this.

"You know, Sister"—the assistant pastor gets up next— "we ain't saying we can't forgive Brother Pemberton. We just saying he's got to confess, ask forgiveness. He needs to beg the church's pardon. This is a serious thing we talking about here. You know you can't come to the Lord with a proud heart now."

His proud heart. Contrition offered to the lowliest of low-lies. How often has he himself said that? This looks sadly like the end of the line with no bus back.

He never planned to do anything. He was old. Set. She was young. Fly. That was all right with him. He figured he understood most of what she had just begun to wonder about, the when-is-it-going-to-happen things that keep people from living. As far as feelings went, he thought he could live with whatever he felt. Not examine it. Not act on it. For the past few months, he was happy just to lend her money, get her to Maurice's when the days were short and cold, pick her up when she couldn't get a cab, and when she could. He felt most like himself when she fussed him out about leaving his doors unlocked. He thinks back to the way they settled with each other, and likes it. He will draw that same picture for the church here. Everyone will understand their wanting to spend Thanksgiving together. He can see Wanda scat-bopping the music inside her while she made a mess of his kitchen.

In a way, he's like a father. He'll point that out, although he isn't sure they will see it as a proper thing. He likes "brother" better. He'll say how he's like a brother. He remembers the day he found her real brother wandering around in Washington Heights. How grateful young Wanda had been then when he brought him home. How happy she will be if they can get her real brother back. He likes "friend" even better. "Boyfriend," "man-friend," her "man." He'll say he's like her brother. Isn't this all useless? No matter what he is to Wanda, or she to him, it will not explain what happened.

Last Saturday night, two days after Thanksgiving, he agreed to pick Wanda up at midnight. He got to Chez de Maurice's early and waited in his car. Years before, he had heard Muddy Waters at Maurice's and though he wasn't interested in going there again, he decided to wait in the coat-check foyer out of the cold. And he was curious.

He heard Wanda talking into a microphone, then the piano and bass starting up, and Wanda singing, *I want a Sunday kind of love, a love to last past Saturday night . . .* her honeyed voice full. To be listening without her knowing it made him uneasy, but he stayed until she finished.

He won't tell that part to the church, they'll be fit to be tied if they know that he went inside the club. They probably want to believe he was drunk, pure and simple.

Once he and Wanda were in his car, she convinced Thomas to drive out to the bluff on County Road to see the mall all done up in Christmas lights.

"I've never seen it before," she said. "They tell me it's a sight. What you say?"

That's where he'll begin his story, their drive to the bluff. Everyone can understand that. They all take their families to see the new lights at the mall after Thanksgiving. He has to start with something normal, or else the whole thing will seem just too low-down.

Thomas drove up the unpaved road expecting to see neon reindeer strung across the roof of the mall, or a gigantic crèche. This was not the kind of thing he enjoyed about Christmas. In the old days, when their rooming house had been full of people, he and Lydia had concentrated on the real meaning of the season, restricted celebrations to dinners and whatever the church designed. But to see excitement animate Wanda's hands as she conducted her own Christmas carol made it worth the drive.

Then she was quiet. "You know, Thomas, used to be I baked and sewed and shopped from Thanksgiving to Christmas Eve. Then took it all down to Osawatomie so Puddin could have some kind of Christmas. They loved to see me coming. But it wasn't really Christmas like we used to have when my father was alive and Puddin was at home."

Was she feeling him out for spending the holidays together? She stretched her arm across his shoulders and let her hand warm the back of his neck.

"Thomas, how old you think I am?"

"Now Wanda," he said. "You know I don't pay no attention to that stuff. I don't go around worrying about how old you are, though maybe I ought to."

"Just tell me," she said.

"Don't make me no difference," he said. But an ancient impulse he thought extinct in him stirred once more. "You old enough, I know that." He wasn't sure what he meant.

"Yes, I am," she said. Then ever so gently, she pressed her hand into the back of his neck.

"I don't know, maybe one of these days somebody I know might want to hook up with me, and we could make us some babies, have us our own family. I'd like to have some real Christmases again. What you think?"

His jaw dropped in surprise. Was she talking about her and him?

"Don't answer," she said. "Think about it a while."

Thomas had never bothered to match his feelings with words, but he was sure he had lived in love with Lydia. This thing with him and Wanda was not what he and Lydia had had. Still, if the truth be known, he would give this girl-of-a-woman anything that was his to give. And what was love if it wasn't a new chance for him, a new time for Wanda, maybe for her brother too? What was love if it wasn't their own dauntless spirits pushing them toward their heart's desire?

The top of the bluff leveled off into a stretch of weeds, frozen and sparkling in his headlights. When he stopped and turned off the lights, everything went pitch. He and Wanda walked toward the edge of the bluff and Thomas saw the mall—doors, windows, high roofs, low roofs, spires, vents, chimneys—all outlined in tiny blue lights.

His eyes were slow to adjust to the dark, and surrounding the mall, there seemed to be one boundless black space. No ground beneath it, no horizon or ceiling of moonless clouds. In that quirk of vision, Thomas saw the mall, with its blue-beaded geometry, transformed. Hanging in the distance, it shimmered.

"Look at that," Wanda said. "A holy city."

It sounds crazy. He knows that they may decide he's evil or dangerous. Maybe he is. But when he tells about that night, they will at least know it was strange to him too. Like a missionary about to hand out his first Bible, he hopes that understanding will come with the telling.

"First Corinthians," Reverend says. "Chapter six, verses nine and ten." Thomas has heard it before, read it aloud himself when members got themselves into trouble with the law or worse. Reverend reads on.

"Do not err; neither fornicators, nor idolaters"—Thomas never noticed until now that fornicators were the first to be mentioned—"nor sodomites, nor thieves . . ." He doesn't listen to the rest. No. He won't deal with fornication when he talks, nothing about right and wrong. He won't even touch what the janitor said he saw. He'll have to get by without going into details.

That night, riding home from the mall through the empty streets, exhilarating calm rang in his head. He looked over at Wanda. She too seemed absorbed, but she noticed before he did that the lights were on at the church. Too late on a Saturday night. Probably the janitor forgot to turn them off. After so strange a night, Thomas half-expected the church to be lit like a way station calling out to them. Likely, too, no one would be there if they entered.

Thomas pressed switches on the wall just inside the door. Although the main lights went out, lights in the entryway stayed on. The glow from the vestibule filtered through windows of the swinging doors into the dark sanctuary. Thomas took Wanda's hand and they walked toward the pulpit. He had nothing particular in mind. Just to be with her there. Perhaps sit with her. Or pray, even. They stood below the pulpit, near the table with its linen cloth and pewter offering trays.

Thomas doesn't remember all of what he said to Wanda, but the words he attempted did not match the gratitude he felt. Then there it was. Her fingers touching his lips to hush him. Everything in him went toward the light behind her eyes. When she received his flesh and bones, he floated in a blue stillness that swallowed and filled him.

"Brother Pemberton," Reverend says, looking down from the pulpit. "You are in the Lord's house. What do you have to say to us?"

Thomas faces them. Most think they know what he has done. They want to know why. What got into him? Some smile the smile of the righteous. They want to know if he thinks he has a prayer, and how much he is suffering.

Thomas stands and looks to Wanda who stands too. She holds out her hand to him. The hand of God bobs, taps gently on the frosted window.

THE LAST
DAY OF
SCHOOL

WHEN THE TWO jet planes made the first pass over the north end of Kansas City, the noise jiggled the windows of our building. In our homeroom on the top floor, most of us bent low to get a look. Mr. Cox flashed one of his expressions that said we would never amount to a hill of beans if we kept this up, then went back to his reading. I collected my books, anticipating the bell that would scatter us to our first-hour classes. It was almost nine o'clock.

Before the government took over Blackwell Aviation Training, we spent many an afternoon listening to the prop planes drone like buzz saws as they went in for grandstand landings at the airfield a few miles from Douglass High. Jets, though, were another story, a new order of power, and they thrilled us.

That morning I wished for short sleeves. September nights often cooled down to the fifties, but the days could still heat up like the scorchers of August. Our windows were raised and whiffs of honeysuckle drifted in. If I listened closely, I could hear scraps of chatter from the neighborhood women in the garden alongside the fence that encircled our stadium. They were busy rooting weeds and harvesting late collards. Again the jets' rumble approached, crescendoed overhead, and died away.

"You people try to do something, just one single thing that is productive today," Mr. Cox said. He stood up from his desk and his lanky frame idled toward the windows. We weren't fooled. He loved to watch fighter planes go through their paces.

To show good faith in the "equal" part of "separate but equal," the state had made our school identical to Horace Mann High, right down to the last sand-colored brick. With all its sections and lawns, our building stretched a whole city block. If you looked out the west windows, you saw the manicured terrace, the wide winding steps and concrete walk that led to our sports field.

To the east, beyond the front lawns and across Emerson Street, Gethsemane Baptist Church stood facing the school and copied our beige brick as if it were an extension. Behind the church, the squat little place with the glass front and the pink neon NETTIE'S DINETTE sign lit up the neighborhood with the promise of something tender smothered in onions. Farther down the block, the Union Hall rose three stories, and that morning if I could have seen that far, I probably would have seen my father there, sitting on the steps, waiting to be called for a job.

Along with Nettie's, the Hall formed a little pocket of city life in our small-town neighborhood of two-story houses with porch swings, pear trees shading tricycles, backyards with trash drums tilting over. Douglass High School presided over this pleasant edge of Rattlebone with such stateliness that whenever out-of-town relatives came to visit, we made certain that we drove past the school on our way out to the lake, or to the real city in Missouri.

The two pilots, probably Air Force cadets, must have been determined to do it right this time. I saw them in the distance, holding formation, streaking along the horizon, wing-to-wing like two bullets across the autumn's serious blue. Then they curved in a wide arc and turned back eastward toward us.

"What were we supposed to do for Algebra II?" John Goodson whispered as he tapped my back with his pencil. I hunched my shoulders. I was not about to start again this year keeping him up on his math.

My eyes were drawn to the planes—two plus signs above the horizon, growing larger, heading in fast. They seemed locked together in their repeat maneuver, flying lower. Mr. Cox glanced out the window. John whispered, "Look at that."

The first-hour bell rang. Instead of joining the happy pandemonium in our halls, a few of us hung back, looking out the windows. In the garden outside, women stood up straight and looked into what strip of sky they could make out. Something in the way they strained to see organized everything around them. The very trees seemed tense. The rest happened in an instant.

They were coming in dangerously low, coming, coming. The pilot in one plane must have been trying to urge the other to pull up. Then the one climbed the sky in a sharp angle, exposing its silver belly to the sun. The other appeared to be locked into a steady plunge. Mr. Cox spun around and yelled, "Run!" The plane had rotated slightly, so that it seemed to be coming broadside straight for us. By the time we considered running, it was too late. The whole room exploded in a fury of glass.

Screams and cries, explosions went on forever. I remember seeing blood on my hands and my ears ringing. Mr. Cox on the floor. I became aware of the fire alarm sounding and a man's voice on the public address telling us which door to use. John and I held on to each other and bolted into a hallway jammed with other students. There seemed to be no way to get outside. Then we were a swarm in confused flight, darting down stairways, a herd of frightened cattle hurtling through the gym and out of the building.

Once outside, I realized that the school was not in flames. People were everywhere—women and men, some of them parents, mostly teachers—calming or calling out, persuading us to run down the slope to the football field. "Hurry!" "That way!" Sirens wailed. We got ourselves to the field. I remember that the ground was very wet. John, Cece, and I locked hands and sat on the grass with others who covered their heads, too stunned or too afraid to look at the fire raging just beyond our school. Suddenly I thought of my father. He might have been at Union Hall. I couldn't focus on what he had said that morning, or even if he had been home when I left the house. From the flames and the dense black smoke, I knew everything on the block, including the Hall, was gone. The three of us sat shivering for the longest time, refugees watching our homeland burn.

Then I saw him. Near the building. Running. It was definitely him. And my mother behind him, running with her arms in the air, yelling something. He reached back for her hand and they ran down the slope toward the field. I stood up. Here was everything mother and father could ever mean, tearing through hell to get to me.

They wrapped me in their arms. With stricken faces, they

said to calm down and stop crying. And no, my father had not gone to Union Hall that morning. He had tried, but he didn't get there.

"Mercy, look at your hand," my mother cried. "Let me see your legs."

My father tied his work kerchief around my hand. "I was about to go to the Hall," he said, "but Pemberton came by. Good thing he did."

"Lord, it's a wonder it didn't get your eyes," my mother mumbled, unsteady now herself. She touched my face. "We've got to take you to the hospital. You need stitches."

About that time police arrived with blankets. More fire engines from Quindaro and Armourdale. Ambulances with oxygen. Wanda and Mr. Pemberton came too, pulling Wanda's brother Puddin along by the hand. Medical people began washing and bandaging, taking us, four or five at a time, into the ambulances.

WHEN THE PLANE came down, it had, mercifully, missed our building by the flimsiest margin. The force of the explosion broke windows, rearranged desks, warped doors. Gethsemane lost its roof. Just yards beyond the church, where the plane finally blew apart, devastation was heaviest. One wall of Nettie's collapsed, and Union Hall burned to ashes, taking with it seven lives. Six other people died in their homes. Metal shaved whole second stories, shredded trees, and set most of the block afire.

The crash became the period at the end of the sentence about life in Rattlebone. After that, nothing was the same. In years to come, people would chronicle events using the crash as a time line. "Before the crash we used to . . ." "Ever since the crash . . ." For some, it remained a tragedy they would never get beyond. For others, it was God's way of putting things right, a new beginning.

Stories of terror and heroism covered the front pages of *The Kansan*. In the wake of the crash, the entire city seemed transformed. At first the pall of loss and grief paralyzed us. We saw the names of the dead, saw their kin at church. Strangers bearing flowers came to funerals and visited hospitals.

Then the focus switched to the survivors and rebuilding. Volunteers began right away on the houses. They put new windows in the school. Horace Mann High donated new, ornate front doors to replace the warped ones at Douglass, their "adopted" school. Every student who attended Douglass became a celebrity with a story to tell. I wore my bandages like medals. People thought, correctly, that this near miss was a miracle. A whole generation of Kansas City's black children had been spared.

At church Reverend asked all the young people who were students at Douglass to come forward and sit in the front row as testimonies of God's grace. Woolworth's on the avenue gave us a ten percent discount at the Colored Only eating counter.

Less than two weeks after the crash, businessmen—black and white—did what people said they should have done long ago. They launched a scholarship fund for the young people of Rattlebone in the name of the men who had lost their lives at Union Hall. Not to be outdone, the Mizells offered to reduce the price of their six-month training course in mortuary science.

Another token of goodwill came from one of the black sororities, the Alpha Kappa Alpha, in Missouri. During study hall one day after school had reopened, Cece and I sat at a long table in the school library and "researched" the comics in *The Kansan*. She showed me the article.

"You ought to do this, Reenie," she said.

"What?"

"Look . . ." and she pointed out the story.

It gave details about the sorority, explaining that they were a black "sisterhood" of teachers who were "dedicated to education for the future," and that they awarded a scholarship every year. It said that ordinarily they were active only in the state of Missouri, but now they were encouraging black girls on the Kansas side of the river to apply. Cece ran her finger down the column.

"Remember her?" she said.

My eyes followed her finger. As I read the words my head cleared like I had suddenly inhaled something pungent and sharp. It said: *Qualified applicants should send letters of request for application to: Miss October Brown, Basileus; 4623 Claremont Avenue; Kansas City, Missouri.*

"Copy the address, why don't you," Cece said. "Who knows, she might even remember you. You know how teachers love to take credit for brainy people, and she always thought you were smart."

I knew not to go into this any deeper; it wouldn't take much for me to feel like an eight-year-old with a lie bump on my tongue. I turned the page.

"I sure would write to her if I were you," Cece said.

I shifted the entire paper to Cece's part of the table and

reached for my stack of books. I didn't need that kind of opportunity.

IN THE THICK of the city's revitalization, my father counted his blessings. The way he told it, on the fortuitous morning of the crash, Mr. Pemberton had given him back his life. He had already left the house on his way to Union Hall when Mr. Pemberton waved him down and held him there on the corner "fumbling with facts and figures" for half an hour.

The deal was that Carl's Cleaners on Fifth Street was closing. The owner had died and the family wanted to sell the business. Mr. Pemberton wanted my father to go in with him and buy it.

"I thought he was crazy. Where would I get that kind of money?" my father said.

But Mr. Pemberton had insisted that at the very least they needed to talk it over. My father put him out of the truck and hightailed it up Seventh Street. That's when he saw the plane go down. The fires and the smoke.

He said, "Right then I felt handpicked. I knew the plane had fallen right on the spot where I would have been standing if Pemberton hadn't come by."

Many a night I listened at the vent upstairs as he sat at the kitchen table telling that story and explaining the practical side of destiny to my mother.

"Pemberton wants us to be partners," he said. "But he don't want to operate the place. He don't need the headache. If I kick in a few hundred and run the place full-time, he'll put down the rest."

My mother was leery. "What you know about running a cleaners, James?" she asked him.

"All I have to know is how to work the presses and how to count money," my father said. "The cleaning part is all by machine. You do it once, you got it."

She wasn't convinced. She brought up how, even during the good months, they could hardly see their way clear. He hinted that if she was so worried, she should get the "ironing customers" that she'd had for ten years to bring their clothes down to the cleaners. He insisted that if my mother helped him every day, they could do it all themselves. "Wouldn't have to hire nobody. We'd probably be making more."

Then my mother got to the part where I thought trouble might lie.

"Me and you living only halfway together as it is," she said. "What makes you think we can both work at the same place?"

My father didn't answer right away. My guess was that he didn't want to wake their sleeping dogs.

Then he told her, "One thing don't have nothing to do with the other. You ain't heard me make a peep, and I ain't heard you complaining either."

"Well, who's going to see to the kids?" she said.

"Don't worry about the kids. They all in school. Reenie can help. People do it all the time."

"I don't know," my mother said. But I could see my father was winning her over. Finally they agreed that they would try it for one year, and my father became part owner of Shorty's New Look Cleaners. When my mother bought the idea, she bought the whole concept, including the ridiculous name.

Those first few weeks had them fighting constantly. One day in the place and I could see why. It had nothing to do with the cleaners itself. A delicate bell above the door announced each customer. That was fine. The chemical they used was not all that unpleasant. Admittedly, giant cones of thread did crowd the front counter a little, along with too many coffee cans crammed with buttons and pinking shears, but they only added to the feeling of easy comfort. My mother had moved her Singer from the house and it fit right in. She could have been inviting me to the YWCA for tea the way she presented the stool for me to sit on and the paper cup of cold soda pop.

However, the pleasant atmosphere evaporated the minute they both started up the pressing machines. As I watched the steam stream out and envelop my mother, I thought of the newsreels from war days, the pictures of factory women working single-mindedly, caught up in the cause. She was all rhythm and speed: lay out a sleeve, press, now the collar, press, now position the shoulder flap, now the tail. My father, on the other hand, though methodical, worked like a reluctant little boy. Even with a flat pair of pants, he would position and reposition a leg, checking it a few times before he lowered the press. Eventually, from what I could gather, they decided to divide the work, and after each of them established a domain, they stopped fighting. Junie and Bea had fits about having to stay with Wanda and Mr. Pemberton every evening until one of us came home. Except for that, we settled comfortably into our new routine.

Around the middle of November every year, the whole area geared up for American Royal Week—for the American Royal Parade in particular. Throughout the state, riding clubs outfitted themselves. Chambers of commerce, farmers, 4-H'ers, even the exclusive country clubs built lavish floats to show off prize steers, beauty queens, and enormous papier-mâché crops. Although we were barred from most of the pageantry, we were invited to the parade. In fact, each year our corps—our school band, together with the drill team, majorettes, and cheerleaders—was the only black anything in the parade. And so, in the undeclared competition of marching bands, we were bent on preserving our reputation for performing the most complicated routines with the tightest precision to the hippest marching music the city had ever heard. And above all else, we had to look good.

All the dazzle that could be drawn from the various combinations of crimson and white, and from the gold trim inside pleats, along seams, and around sleeves, was enhanced by the expertise of my father and mother and their now-excellent enterprise. That November, partly because I was a Douglass student, and partly because my father was a "new businessman," our shop was chosen to clean and repair all the uniforms. And we did it. Beautifully.

I loved our new status. You would have thought we were rich the way John and Cece teased me about the pink Cadillac my father was sure to buy. Maybe it wouldn't be a Cadillac, but my parents now had a savings account at the bank. We were sure to have a car before we got another truck.

People I had never seen before recognized me on the bus.

"You must be Shorty's daughter, I can see it in your face," they'd say. "Wilson, from the cleaners, right?"

We were fast becoming "established," and for a change nothing stood in our way. I could imagine myself waving college brochures with the best of them at school. I couldn't believe I had been so timid before, trembling over a name on a piece of paper, afraid to write the letter that could get me a scholarship. What could they do to me?

Without the least hesitation now, I sent for an application, and when it arrived, I filled it out, signed it, and sent it to Miss October Brown.

As THE HOLIDAYS approached, to my father's delight, business doubled. We had a good Christmas. One afternoon I walked the seven blocks in the snow to the cleaners just to take in how far we had come. Dramatic flourishes across the front window now announced my father's ownership in gold, trimmed in black. Through the glass I saw the two of them, my mother chatting while she sat on the stool and hemmed a pair of pants, my father with his back to the window, nailing up new Sheetrock on one of the back walls. He turned and said something to her. She paused in her sewing, laughed in the way she had of wagging her head, and tossed him a measuring tape. When she sat down again she noticed me. I waved and went on home.

By the time we finished dinner that same evening and I had done the dishes, they had settled at the table with the day's receipts. My mother clicked away on the adding machine while my father went over figures in their ledger.

"This right?" he said and turned the book around for her to see.

"Yeah. Remember we said we'd change it next time?"

"Right," he said, and continued with his pencil.

"Guess what Maizy Carpenter told me," my mother said to him, and he looked up.

My mother clicked the keys a few more times and cranked the arm of the adding machine.

"She takes her drapes and slipcovers uptown and pays her weight in gold to have 'em done," she said.

"This time next year we ought to have a down payment on some new equipment," my father said.

"You reading my mind," my mother said. She raised her eyebrows and rubbed her fingers together as the sign of money to be had. "Maizy could be ours . . ."

At such times I noted that working together had changed them. They regarded each other with more good humor, casually, without defense. Yet when the night grew late, they fell back to the habitual estrangement of separate bedrooms, alone and apart. I wondered when that too would change.

At this point in my senior year of high school I understood some things. For one, what was past was past. Life for my parents was better now; they had more security. Perhaps they could also create something better between them. Something softer. Romance maybe.

From my perspective, opportunity flaunted itself every day. My father need only show a little more affection. My mother liked delicate things like the heart-shaped porcelain dish where she kept her earrings. And she had a birthday coming. I played around with the idea of suggesting to my father that he get her something with lace. It couldn't be a one-way street, either. My mother knew very well how much he liked jazz records. I could remember the times she had made lemon cake from scratch and dared us to touch it until he had had a piece. Little things, but special. This was what they needed.

The first time my father dropped my mother off without coming inside, I thought little of it. She seemed unconcerned and said he had to go back to the shop. A storm had been predicted, and when it began to snow I expected him to be late. When it was still snowing the next morning and it was clear that he had not been home all night, I worried.

"I thought I told you," she said. "He stayed down at the shop. Wasn't no need to come home in the middle of the night just to go back this morning. I'm fixing some breakfast to take down there." Sure enough, she packed breakfast and lunch for him, and he shoveled his way to our door to pick her up.

The next evening when they came home, he stayed only to have dinner, get a change of clothes and a few things out of his toolbox, and he was off again.

"Haven't you seen the place upstairs yet?" she said. "I thought we showed it to you. It's a nice little apartment up there, but it needs plaster and a paint job."

I didn't even know they owned the upstairs. I asked if they were going to rent it out when it was finished.

"We'll see," my mother said.

This was in February. "Down in the hole of winter," my mother called it. One night in the middle of the week, she fixed us a Sunday meal—pork chops and fried apples with all the trimmings. Splurging, I figured, because winter was dull and prosperity had knocked on our door.

After the pork chops and before the hand-packed Velvet Freeze with chocolate sauce, Junie asked, "Why are we having all this?" as if we were being silly and being sensible had just occurred to him.

For the briefest of seconds, my father's eyes met my mother's and they both looked away. Something was wrong.

"Since when don't you want a little ice cream?" she said to Junie. "Some days need a little sprucin up."

Right then, I wanted to know what she meant, but we all went on eating dessert with my mother, father, and Bea making chitchat. My father finished first and got up to leave the table.

Junie said to him, "Daddy, you going back down to the cleaners tonight?"

"Yeah," my father said and went on into the front room. I heard him throw himself down on the sofa. "But not right this minute," he yelled to Junie.

"Why? Why do you have to go back?"

Bea echoed, "Yeah, why?"

"That's enough," my mother said. "Y'all stop all the racket and finish eating."

My father came back to the kitchen doorway. "It's okay, Pearl," he said. "Ain't no need to wait no longer."

"Wait for what?" I asked.

"Let's all sit down in the front room, then," my mother said. "No need in making no big to-do at the table."

We all went to the front room. My father sat down on the sofa and rubbed his hands together. We sat down too. I knew that in the next moment some sweet part of our lives was going to turn sour.

My father looked first at my mother, then at us, then sailed right through it.

"Me and your mamma decided we'd like to live apart from now on, so I'm going to be living up over the cleaners and she's going to be staying here with y'all."

Nobody made a sound.

Then Bea hugged my mother's arm. "Nobody else's mother has to live by herself," she said.

"Well, look at Mrs. Coles," my mother said, making light.

"I knew it!" Junie said. He breathed hard, tuning up.

"Hey, June Bug," my father said. "How you think you're gonna like coming down on Friday nights and me and you going to get us some ribs?"

I could hardly believe it. I looked at them with their new united front.

"So you all are getting a divorce?" I asked them.

The look on their faces said I was right.

"We'll see," my mother said.

"What's there to see?" I croaked.

"That's enough, Irene," my mother said. "You just calm down before you get these children upset."

Because no more words could form themselves right then, I stood up and glared at them.

"Sit down, Irene," my father said.

I could hardly stand still for the torture in my chest.

"Girl, you better sit down now, this is between me and your daddy." She looked at him for support.

He said weakly, "Sit down, Reenie. Me and your mamma already worked this all out."

I could feel a big ugly sound welling in my throat, and I ran upstairs.

That evening they coaxed Junie and Bea into helping pack more of my father's things and the four of them went to see the apartment where he would live. Just like that, our family was over.

EARLY IN MARCH, amid all this change, my letter of invitation arrived from the Alpha Kappa Alpha sorority. They wanted me to come for an interview a week later at Central High School in Missouri. I folded the letter. How could I back out now?

On the day of the interview, ominously enough, it began to snow a long wet snow. The ordeal of getting overtown to Missouri by bus gave me several chances to wonder why I should so blatantly tempt fate.

I waited outside the door of the office and saw a self-assured young woman leave before a Miss Boswell came out to get me. Miss Brown was one of the other three committee members who greeted me. Except for the fact that her vitiligo had spread to her neck and hands, she looked as I remembered her—a stylish and slender dark woman with a camel's prance and wild hair.

A gleaming tea service stood on a silver tray in the middle of the desk, and the women sat in chairs scattered over the office.

"Would you like some hot cocoa, Irene?" Miss Boswell asked. I declined the cocoa, but said I would like a cookie. That was a mistake. Once I took it, I had to bite it, chew it, and wipe crumbs off my face. One of the women hung my coat on the coat rack and admired my skirt. Miss Boswell told me to have a seat in the easy chair set like an inquisitor's device in the middle of the room. They all drank cocoa. They asked me, and between swallows I told them, about my bus trip overtown.

Miss Brown didn't chat. Instead, her interest seemed fixed on my application.

"First, let me just say that this is the informal part of the process of selecting our girls every year," she said. "So relax, Irene, nobody's writing anything down." She smiled at me. "These are my sorors, Miss Cates, Mrs. Bracken, and of course Miss Boswell."

I said "How do you do" to each of them. Miss Cates began.

"Talk a little bit about yourself, Irene, how you're doing in school, your hobbies, that sort of thing."

It was all there on the application, but I told them about my interests in drama and math. Miss Brown merely smiled. They asked me about my brother and Bea, and if we went to church. Nothing direct about my parents.

"Tell us, Irene, in your own words, why do you think you should have this scholarship?"

I had written what I considered an outstanding paragraph about why I wanted to go to college, but looking into their expectant faces, I couldn't remember a word of it. I only knew that I wanted some kind of future somewhere. I wasn't sure that I really answered the question, but I managed to convey that surviving the crash had made me think about my own future. That because of it, I had learned a lot about myself and other people. And that I believed I would prove myself worthy of their reward. Something like that.

They nodded approval as I spoke and I assumed that they were not disappointed. As we chatted about what subjects I might pursue in college, I felt relief. It was not as difficult as I had feared. Miss Boswell got up to get my coat and said that I would hear from them in a few weeks, indicating that the interview was over.

"One final thing," Miss Brown said. "I'd like to ask you, Irene, if you had to name your worst flaw, what would it be?"

Miss Cates interjected, "It doesn't have to be something dreadfully wrong or ugly, Irene. Just something you'd like to work on."

I felt ambushed. Quickly I went down the mental list of the Ten Commandments. Did she want me to say *lying*? I feared God, honored my parents, I'd never kill or steal. Covetousness was the only commandment I could think of that I could break and still be a decent person.

"I guess it would be envy," I said. "Wanting what somebody else has. I guess that's what I would work on."

"Fine, fine," Miss Cates said. I sensed that anything I said would have been fine with her. Miss Brown looked amused and helped me into my coat. As she walked me to the door, she put her arm around my shoulders.

"You always were a crackerjack, Irene," she said. "You'll do well, no matter what."

On the bus, going home, I thought about her words. What did she mean when she said, "No matter what"?

THE HARD WINTER held through the Easter holiday in late March. Yet more and more, a west wind softened the bitter edge of the cold. And then there were the robins. Foolish birds. Their song should really have been a complaint; they had returned to a desert of snow. Still, they managed to find an occasional spot of ground soft enough to yield a worm or two.

Perhaps I needed to know that a thaw was coming before I could finally go to visit my father. The cold evening that I walked to his place, I counted up the days. It had been more than six weeks.

I hadn't expected the place to be so nice. Nicer than our house. Nicer than the place Wanda used to have. It was a room, with an alcove bedroom and a tiny bath. It smelled like paint, and everything was so clean. So shiny! Even the wooden floor. My father was nervous, but he was excited, too. "Look at this." He had a bright blue studio couch with two pillows. The biggest thing in the whole place was his console—record player *and* radio. AM *and* FM. And he had a shelf now for all his records. "Did you see these?" All his dishes matched, and he even had highball glasses. In the little refrigerator-freezer he had one small pint of ice cream.

I could see that he was happy. I had to admit that I felt a little twinge of happiness for him. But as soon as I did, I began to wonder about my mother: perhaps he had actually abandoned her, perhaps she was protecting him, suffering in proud silence.

"And just who do you think saw to it that he got that furniture and stuff so he could move up there?" my mother said when I asked her about it. "Chile, don't you worry 'bout your mamma. She's always gonna get what she needs." A whole minute passed before she winked and added, "And we ain't goin another-further into that!"

Exactly one month after my interview, the letter arrived. Alpha Kappa Alpha. I took it immediately to my room, and laid it on my bed. Not yet. I went down and opened a can of salmon to start croquettes for dinner. I chopped onions. I crushed crackers with the rolling pin. Junie and Bea came in and rifled the refrigerator. I peeled potatoes and put them on to boil. I couldn't wait. Upstairs again, I opened the letter. "Congratulations," it said.

THEY WERE JUNIORS. All girls. They encircled us like angels shepherding the redeemed into the Promised Land. In white dresses they formed their traditional daisy chain around the graduating senior class and walked us en masse onto the football field, now set with rows of wooden folding chairs. Already the rest of the student body of Douglass High filled the stone stair-step bleachers. The promise of the feast to come wafted our way on smoke from the barbecue drums at the far end of the field.

The day wore its widest blue sky and wrapped itself in the scent of a million flowerings. From my seat in the first row with the others who would receive scholarships, I could see men finishing the roof of Gethsemane. Their hammers pumped silent blows that registered a moment later on our ears.

In my mind's eye I saw what I had seen so many times when I turned the corner where Gethsemane stood and followed the street for seven blocks to the cleaners now called Wilson's Cleaning and Tailoring: my father sorting while my mother ran the presses for the one-day-service shirts; my mother bending over him to examine a tiny moth hole that required an extra charge if she fixed it; him pouring half a Nehi orange soda pop into a cup with ice cubes and setting it on the sewing machine for her, then drinking the rest himself. Two contented people. Then at six o'clock my mother all but skipping out the door to her new worn-out '49 Ford that she drove like a bucking horse, and that she liked "better than all y'all put together," and she loved us a lot.

As I looked up at the suddenly quiet bleachers, at the faces turned toward us, the band started up. The Daisy Chain Girls began to serenade us with their version of "Thanks for the Memory." A jet plane flew over, drowning them out for a moment, but they came back strong. On the morning breeze the melody made its way throughout the whole of Rattlebone. The awards ceremony had begun.